Seasons of Death

Michael C

About the author

Freelance photojournalist Mike Charity, has been involved with newspaper and television news since the late 1950s.

Learning his craft at Derek Evans' photo agency in Hereford, Mike moved to Cheltenham in 1963 to start his own agency and established himself with Fleet Street picture editors as 'Charity of Cheltenham'.

He has covered hundreds of news stories in the UK, both for publications and television ranging from the 1966 Aberfan disaster in Wales to journeys with British forces to trouble spots in Belfast,

Borneo and Aden. Later assignments included the 1983-5 famine in Ethiopia, the aftermath of the Romanian revolution and work for TV with a medical charity in Sierra Leone.

Mike has always had a passionate interest in factual crime and has produced many features on current and past criminals for specialist magazines. On two occasions he has been invited as a guest speaker at annual Crime Writers' Association seminars.

Of all the photographic assignments Mike has covered for news organisations, two are indelibly printed in his mind—the famine in Ethiopia and Gloucester's Cromwell Street murders, his longest-ever job.

Central TV News booked him on 24th February 1994—day 3 of police activity at Fred and Rose West's home. Three months later he was still filming unfolding events at Cromwell Street and other sites involved in the enquiry, constantly feeding material to Central's news desk.

His camera rolled when Fred West committed suicide, again when judge and jury visited 25 Cromwell Street during the Rose West trial and again when she was sentenced at Winchester Crown Court. Finally he returned again to Cromwell Street when the infamous property Number 25, was demolished.

Now in his 70s, Mike is still taking photographs and writing features.

All photographs by Mike Charity - unless otherwise stated.

Book cover image illustrates Fingerpost Field, Kempley on the Gloucestershire-Herefordshire border near the village of Much Marcle, where police finally unearthed the body of Fred West's victim, Anna McFall

PublishNation, London
www.publishnation.co.uk

Missing people

In February 1994, resources at the charity National Missing Persons Helpline (NMPH) were stretched to the limit by news of events at 25 Cromwell Street, Gloucester. Many callers reported missing relatives for the first time, even though some had vanished ten years before. Distressed families, already in touch with the charity, called again, fearing that their missing relative might figure in the new police investigation. With triple the usual number of enquiries, extra volunteers were called in to man the helpline.

Gloucestershire police also contacted the charity, seeking help in identifying the bodies discovered in the house and garden of Fred and Rose West. Their initial interest was in women reported missing from Worcestershire and Gloucestershire during the 1970s and 1980s. The police came up with 390 names, among them Alison Chambers and Carol Cooper, who were both later identified as Cromwell Street victims. In turn, details obtained by the police during many interviews with Fred West were passed to NMPH's database, the outcome confirming that missing teenager Juanita Mott had lost her life at Cromwell Street. Among so much heartbreak, there was at least some good news in that 110 non-victim families were reunited—an achievement brought about by the charity in under two months. NMPH was subsequently honoured that HRH The Duchess of Gloucester GCVO, accepted the role of Patron and continues to attend events on behalf of the charity, now named Missing People while also raising the morale of staff and volunteers with regular visits to their London headquarters. Having learned about the charity and the valuable help they gave to the Gloucestershire police investigation, I felt this remarkable organisation was deserving of support so, should this book enjoy some modest success, a portion of the royalties will be donated towards the good works of Missing People.
Mike Charity

To our son Daniel, who is following in his father's photoprints with some success in the hectic world of national newspapers, once collectively known as 'Fleet Street'. His current global assignments on behalf of *The Sun* newspaper make my earlier efforts seem as day-trips by comparison. With much love and appreciation to Gillian my wife and partner, who coped admirably and understandingly with my constant absence and late homecomings during the police enquiry's frantic first year on the Frederick and Rosemary West investigation.

Preface

As you read this, two decades have passed since the police officers first door-knocked at 25 Cromwell Street, Gloucester, the home of Fred and Rose West, the rat-a-tat setting off a chain reaction which echoed around the world.

The shock horror discoveries in house and garden of the sombre Victorian property, continued with further diabolical revelations at another city property and in two fields on the Gloucestershire/Herefordshire borders. The findings created a powerful media magnet attracting waves of journalists, photographers and television crews from this and other countries, all of whom fetched up at the dismal terraced house that would become described by the press as, 'The House Of Horrors'.

Though known colloquially as 'The Cromwell Street Inquiry', police activities encompassed 25 Midland Road, two fields near the village of Much Marcle in Herefordshire, Gloucester police station, magistrates' court and a variety of other venues that arose during the police proceedings over a period of two and half years.

I covered these astounding times for Central Television News from February 26th 1994 (day three of inquiry) until Rose West's trial at Winchester Crown Court in November 1995, followed by the demolition of 25 Cromwell Street, when it was erased from Gloucester's landscape in 1996. In fairness to others, I must make the point I was by no means the only, or best, cameraman working on the investigation coverage. Central TV regularly brought in extra staff cameramen to film the multitude of news angles and interviews associated with the police activities. But somehow during the initial days of the inquiry I became 'embedded' in the district, accepted by the locals and tolerated by the law. This aided the making of contacts and acquaintances who in providing valuable tip-offs, led to the newsdesk booking me daily to keep the glass eye on happenings and my ear to the ground. When finally it was all over, it appeared I had spent more time than any other cameraman or journalist within the pale of Cromwell Street, during the two-and-a-half year epic investigation.

The reason for writing this book is not to re-hash the gruesome goings on at 25 Cromwell Street, this has been underlined by both tabloid and television other books in detail enough. What I have tried to portray are the behind-the-scene situations of media folk when confronted with such an enormous news story. The mix of artfulness, dexterity, determination and sheer bloodymindedness employed by reporters, photographers and television presenters, in overcoming police restrictions and neighbourly resistance to obtain images, facts and sometimes fiction, during such a maelstrom.

When a big news story breaks 'being there' is a strong driving force to all in the news media camp, seeing it through to the end is another, though the latter is not always possible. Mysteries often remain hanging in the air for years, decades even. Their doing so stirs some journalists into returning each year, not just to the story but to its very source, an annual pilgrimage in hope of more revelations, further facts, the almost futile dream of being able to type that final chapter.

Threading through the book is such a story. The 1968 mystery disappearance of Gloucester teenager, Mary Bastholm. The police file on Mary is still open —even Scotland Yard were unable to solve the case. In later chapters I write of local reporter, Hugh Worsnip. We were both involved in the Mary Bastholm story and like me, Hugh has spent the last 46 years wondering of her whereabouts and fate. We both still have in our minds futile dreams of new information, fresh facts enabling us to type Mary's final chapter. We are both sure we came near to closure twenty years ago—oh, so close —when police knocked on the door of Fredrick Walter Stephen West.

Watching

The rubber-clad police frogman was gently lowered by his colleagues into the well of the unimposing semi-detached Victorian house. The man's task was not a pleasant one. In the dark, foul-smelling confines of the long-abandoned domestic watering hole, he was searching, not for drugs or the abandoned proceeds of robbery, but for signs of human remains. Anxiously watching the unfolding scene, Detective Superintendent John Bennett, the officer in charge of the case, kept his professional eye on the diver as he slid under the water. He knew from personal experience the problems and dangers in such an exercise having been, some twenty-six years previously, a member of the very same sub-aqua team. Back then, a young, ambitious policeman, he was part of the biggest police investigation undertaken in the county. The probe was headed by Detective Superintendent Bill Marchant, brought in from Scotland Yard, adding years of craft to the detectives in that freezing snow-laden month of January 1968, in their search to find a missing sixteen-year-old Gloucester girl, Mary Bastholm.

The pretty teenager had set out on the bitterly cold evening of Saturday January 6th, to catch a bus to her boyfriend's home some three miles away in the village of Quedgeley. The couple had planned a cosy fireside night where, on the roll of a dice, they would buy and sell chunks of London real estate, 'Pass Go'. 'Obtain Tax Rebates'. 'Collect Rent' or 'Go To Jail'.

But the game of Monopoly, invented in capitalist America but banned in Russia, China and Cuba, would not to be played in England that night by the two sweethearts. Mary was last seen waiting at a bus stop in Gloucester's Bristol Road by a witness who estimated the time as around 8pm The only other clue to her being there, a few items from her favourite game left scattered in the snow. Mary didn't arrive for her Quedgeley tryst, neither family nor boyfriend saw her again. Mary Bastholm disappeared from the face of the earth. Over 130 members of the Gloucestershire County police force were seconded to the search for the missing teenager and the hunt was now being treated as murder by the detectives, even though no body had been found.

The search teams probed lay-bys, garden sheds, abandoned buildings and vast tracts of snow-swept land. The sub-aqua squad broke the ice canal covered ice floes and trawled the frozen depths as the search continued, both around the city and in the county, with the aid of tracker dogs and helicopters. But despite the huge police commitment and the added skills of the Scotland Yard team, the force was unable to find, alive or dead, the missing girl whose name was now on everyone's tongue, Mary Bastholm. As if a melting flake of snow, she had vanished into the cold air. During the search for Mary, I had filmed in black and white using a 16 mm clockwork Bolex camera for ATV News, police frogman Bennett and his colleagues in action. Over a quarter of a century later, in the strange way history and news stories occasionally repeat themselves, I was filming him again, this time with state-of-the-art video equipment in full colour and instant sound. He was no longer a constable or active member of the sub- aqua team but now a senior police officer in charge of his own case, heading the gruesome Cromwell Street inquiry in Gloucester's city centre.

The remains of nine young women had already been discovered by his team at the tabloid-tagged 'House of Horrors' and the search of the disused well was the final task left, before sealing up the infamous house and moving on to other potential crime locations that held links to Fred and Rose West.

Watching his officer descend into the dark waterway hole, it was inevitable the scene would evoke memories of his former frogman days and the desperate hunt during that freezing winter of 1968 for the Gloucester teenager. Now, supremo of an inquiry that was fast becoming one of Great Britain's biggest murder investigations, his thoughts throughout the coming months would be brought again and again to consider the disappearance of Mary Bastholm. Could there now possibly be a link to his current inquiries? Several of the

Cromwell Street victims' last movements echoed those of Mary's known final journey. Like her, they set out to catch a bus or hitch a lift. Like her, they never reached their destination.

The point cannot have escaped the detective's logical thinking. It must have churned over in Bennett's mind that Mary may have been an early victim of Fred West. Was it possible that, when this terrible affair was brought to its conclusion, the detective would also be able to solve the riddle of the missing sixteen-year-old?

Street of ink

Towards the end of 1993, Fleet Street had all but passed away. The once great river of ink was drying up, its roaring presses almost silent. The most exciting street in London, home to the Fourth Estate, had been asset-stripped out of existence. Murdoch's titles had already decamped to Fortress Wapping, the move heralding the electronic gadgetry that would replace the typewriter and revolutionise news-gathering to the point where other nationals had no choice but to follow. The *Daily Telegraph* moved out of its period-piece baronial edifice for Canada Wharf, the *Daily Express* vacated their smoke-glazed building, wickedly named by staff, 'The Black Lubianka', to set up shop in Blackfriars.

Despite the shock of the new, muffled phones, near silent computer keys fingered over by non-smoking scribes, the *Express* at least made one concession to journalistic convention—a well-stocked bar on the ground floor of their Blackfriars headquarters! Else for the old school, things would never be the same again. Computers replaced iron-framed typewriters, mobile phones took over from pagers, the days of scribbled notes on the backs of fag packets long gone. Against this background of media turmoil, shuffled balance sheets, stringent budgets, 1993 slid into the New Year.

Daily diaries

Most in the media looked forward to the end of the festive season, one can take only so much Christmas and New Year cheer—it soon goes stale. We also looked forward to getting back to normal, bacon rolls in steamy-windowed cafés, meetings with colleagues over coffee or a pint in the pub, knowing again what day it was and when a proper week began.

In Gloucestershire, as in other towns and cities at the start of New Year, the local papers, regional television and radio channels, all pencil into their diaries the 'hardy annual' assignments for the coming months. Times and dates for the likely dramatic Severn Bore tides, more often than not a damp squib, Cheltenham's Gold Cup meeting, pancake day races, Easter egg capers, Bourton-on-the-Water's river football, the royalty-packed horse trials at Badminton.

Curiously, hills feature strongly in news-gathers' diaries: the bone-breaking madness of cheese-rolling on Cooper's Hill, the ancient sunrise custom of May Day dawn dance and song on top of May Hill, the annual crazy shin-kicking competitions of the 'Cotswold Olimpic Games' on Dover's Hill at Chipping Campden, created in 1612. More modern-day adventures are made by car and driver speeding around the hairpin bends and steep slopes of Prescott hill climb events. Veteran and vintage automobiles risk dents and worse in their race to beat the clock. Yes, the hills of Gloucestershire are very much alive, but there's not much sound of music.

These events come round with regular monotony, nevertheless creating bread-and-butter work for scribes and snappers alike. Sandwiched hopefully between these 'norms' is the wish all of newsmen—the arrival of a 'scoop'—or in today's mediaspeak, an 'exclusive'. An out-of-the-blue happening that will not only grab the headlines but give street vendors the opportunity to shout, 'read all about it'.

A story with legs that will run and run. A scandal perhaps: 'vicar elopes with beauty queen', or a disaster: 'chemical explosion pollutes village'. No decent media folk wish ill to befall anyone but should fate, as it so often does, strike its cruel blow anywhere, maybe it could fall within their bailiwick! As 1994 loomed, we readied for events to come but none of us, callow or experienced, were ready for the horrific outcome that would unfold, a happening that would put the City of Gloucester on a map of such gruesome scale it would defy human comprehension.

Season of death

February 24th, a Thursday, began the same as all previous post-Christmas days, morning phone calls to colleagues and contacts, followed by calls to police, fire and ambulance. Things were quiet in our patch. Gloucester and County News Service, run by two journalists, John Hawkins and Jeff Weaver, mentioned a rumour of police activity in the city and were checking it out, otherwise it seemed to be a flat news day. Made a call to the Gloucester base of Central Television offering my services but they were not needed, they too were short on stories, with cameramen kicking their heels. This negative trend, like the rain, appeared set for the day.

Gloucester and County News called back: "police at a house in Cromwell Street, kids have reported a body in a garden—it's not being taken seriously". A Friday morning check call revealed more of the same. Police had returned to the Gloucester garden but there was no further news regarding their activities. It appeared to be a repeat of the previous day—pouring rain and muddied bobbies. Again it was to be an office-bound day.

Quite early on Saturday morning, Central Television's newsdesk called wanting film coverage at Cromwell Street: "nothing happening there of any note, keep an eye on it just in case". Driving towards Gloucester, I was not to know this was to be the first of many daily journeys to the city, journeys that would take up a whole season of visits to Cromwell Street.

The unremarkable Victorian houses south of Gloucester that make up Cromwell Street, have in many cases have seen better times. The few owner-occupiers still living there are land-locked in a sea of bedsits and flats carved out of the rambling properties to provide dwellings for students, dole folk, single parents and the sad of our society. The terraced properties, unfortunately similar to so many in urban England, house a mix of folk who, with resigned reticence, face local aggression and criminal behaviour in the only way they know—by looking the other way, turning the other cheek, scuttling inside, locking the door, closing the curtains and shutting out the outside world.

Most of the windows in Cromwell Street have their curtains drawn as if there has been a death in the households.

It was still pouring with rain when I fetched up at the mud-splattered back garden, a plot that was rapidly turning into a quagmire of major proportions. The police 'support group' were battling against the odds as their boots sunk into the mud and shovels jammed in the cloying soil. A soaking of local press were on hand watching the garden-digging bobbies probe the sodden earth in their search for they-knew-not-what.

The force press officer, Inspector David Morgan, was also there, parrying questions with low-key answers—things were just routine, they were not expecting dramatic developments. But things are not always as they appear and this was very much the case on the morning of Saturday 26th February when I was drafted in by Central TV. What was being artfully hidden from the media by detectives were the revelations brought about by their activities over the past thirty-six hours.

When Fred West had returned home from work on the Thursday evening, after police left the scene on that first day of digging, he voluntarily went to Gloucester police station where he was interviewed by Detective Constable Hazel Savage regarding the disappearance of his daughter, Heather. During the interview he mentioned that he had seen Heather recently in Birmingham. The same evening, Rose West was home in the first-floor lounge, answering detectives' questions into a recording machine.

At around 9.30pm that Thursday night, West left the police station, returning home a free man. Early the next morning the 'support group' were again toiling away in the back garden watched by the local media who decided this was the only place to be. At about 11am, detectives quietly entered 25 Cromwell Street via the front door to interview Fred and Rose West. Later, unseen by the press, Fred West was taken to a CID car parked in front of the house. In the vehicle, he admitted Heather was in the garden but 'the police are looking in the wrong place'.

Detective Constable Savage arrested Frederick West, as he sat in their car, for the murder of his daughter, then he was quickly driven away to be detained at Gloucester police station.

By midday, Rose West, also in the frame, was arrested on suspicion of the murder of Heather by Detective Sergeant Onions and taken to Cheltenham police station. The couple were intensively questioned at various times throughout that day and evening at the Gloucester and Cheltenham police stations, with Rosemary West offering only total denial that she was guilty of killing her daughter. Under the cover of winter darkness that evening, Fred West was taken back to his home by detectives, where in the garden he roughly indicated the place of his daughter's burial, before returning to the station cells.

Saturday morning (Feb 26th) after what must have been a restless night behind bars, West was to face more questions. This time he stunned the interviewing detectives by retracting his previous admission of murder. In a second interview at 2pm that afternoon he still maintained his innocence.

It took a third time of questioning at 4.30pm that day, just after human remains were discovered in the garden, before Fred West again admitted to killing his daughter Heather. He was, no doubt, playing cat-and-mouse with his interrogators while the detectives were doing the same with the media.

They had manoeuvred all activity to focus on the Cromwell Street back garden, which left the front of the house uncovered by the press. Thus newspaper and TV cameras missed the arrests of both Fred and Rose West as well as Fred's nocturnal return to the garden with detectives (though to be fair, he may not have been spotted anyway, as he was disguised in 'support group' overalls). The police were keeping things close to their chests in making no mention of their current revelations. The press were kept in the cold in more ways than one, a situation that suited the tight-lipped detectives. Right up until 4pm on my first day there, it had been a watch-and-wait scenario, when suddenly the garden went quiet.

We sensed something serious was happening on seeing the silent huddle of police officers hunched over a hole in the earth. This location was different to the one indicated by West the previous night. Here in another area of the garden, officers had revealed a bone which, when examined by Home Office pathologist, Bernard Knight at Gloucester police station was confirmed to be a human femur (thigh bone).

Later, facing a battery of flashguns, Professor Knight visited the Wests' garden to inspect further remains that had been discovered at the spot Fred West had pointed out the previous night. They were in fact Heather West's remains, complete with both femurs. The shocking discovery of a *third* thigh bone meant there was every reason to believe another body was beneath the earth. West was again questioned during that Saturday evening regarding the third femur and admitted to killing and burying a woman he named as

Shirley Robinson. Around 9pm the same night under further questioning, he admitted also strangling a girl he called Alison Chambers.

Just three days had elapsed since the initial digging at the Wests' home and already police had found his daughter's body, revealed more human remains and now had West's admission he had killed and buried two more girls in the plot of land.

Now the media—other than the police facility of being allowed to photograph the garden scene and the occasional issued hand-me-down-quotes from police press officers—had something to go on, something for the journalists to dig at, as well as the police. Things had altered, human remains had been unearthed. What at the outset had been considered a hoax, children's tittle-tattle, a kiddie's fantasy, was now deadly serious.

The developing situation was explained to Central TV's newsroom. A dispatch rider would collect the tapes for the evening's bulletin. I was to stay at the scene. We now pictured the arrival of top brass officers, scenes of crime specialists—even the police shift changes provided material for the ever-hungry belly of television news.

With events unfolding apace, the atmosphere between police and press took on a new form. We wanted to know and to see—they did not want to tell or show. This is a natural state of affairs in circumstances so macabre, one that is accepted when confronting the 'Old Bill'. Where we had first been tolerably welcome on the edge of the garden, now we were unwanted. Barriers were erected to cut off the path to the rear of the soon-to-be-Christened 'House of Horrors'. Police patrolled the front and rear entrances to keep out the prying eyes and lenses of press and public. Pushed back with no view of the rapidly-increasing police activity, we retreated into St Michael's Square, a large quadrangle of Edwardian properties that surround an NCP car park. A tract of land that, in its heyday, would have provided a private, lawned park to the imposing houses, rather than a tarmac hard-standing for vehicles. To the north side of the square the three-storey buildings conveniently overlooked the rear gardens of Cromwell Street.

The magic word 'television' gave us entry to the ground floor levels, affording better views of Fred and Rose West's back garden, allowing our lens to focus on the rising police-made hills of earth being excavated from a patch of soil that once was the playground of children.

As any major police inquiry develops, local folk are always ready for a casual doorstep chat with reporters. Having witnessed the flurry of police activity, they are hungry for news, a whiff of gossip, a hint of detail. In return for this, the reporter hopes for a sackful of knowledge. They trade on the doorstep, fact for gossip. For every householder's question, there will be ten from the scribe. The odd bit of news from the reporter's lips will be swapped for the who? why? what? where? when? concerning the people and property under scrutiny by the law. Two or three such rat-a-tats will be converted into several column inches in tomorrow's editions.

The local folk will be fed a few scraps of detail to mull and gossip over—not a lot, but it makes a change from Coronation Street.

The journalist's time-honoured art of door-knocking, even before the arrests in the terrace, had come up trumps, revealing identities and more, about the inhabitants of 25 Cromwell Street. The names of Frederick Stephen Walter West and Rosemary Pauline West, were now in their notepads. Their names would soon be on billboards, in headlines, on the lips of Gloucester folk. Fred and Rose West, their two names and their house number, 25 Cromwell Street, destined to soon be on the lips of the world.

In that very first week of mayhem, with timing that left a lot to be desired, one householder was preparing to sell his property. The estate agent's For Sale sign hung at the front entrance just a couple of doors away from the Wests' abode. The owner was interviewed by

TV and newspapers, affording what would, in normal circumstances, be fabulous free publicity to a vendor. But circumstances were not normal in Cromwell Street. Already low down on the agents' lists of desirable districts, the area had plummeted in esteem as the depths of Fred and Rose West's depravity unfolded.

Two years later the billboard would still be swaying optimistically in the breeze.

Conference season

The first formal Cromwell Street press conference given by John Bennett was held in the Gloucester city police station canteen. A low-key event attended by local scribes and snappers, regional radio and TV stations with the usual London agencies and a couple of Bristol-based national journalists. During the conference, the police confirmed that three bodies had so far been recovered from the garden of 25 Cromwell Street. They were identified at Heather West, Alison Chambers and Shirley Robinson.

When all questions and interviews were over, my colleague Les Leach, a BBC Bristol Points West cameraman, with whom I had worked on many stories, met up to discuss the police revelations. We both wondered if light might now be thrown on the case of missing Gloucester teenager, Mary Bastholm and later disappearance of Cheltenham's Lucy Partington who, like Mary, also vanished from a bus stop, never to be seen again.

We approached the Detective Superintendent and casually asked 'off the record' if, after all these years, the two missing girls might be connected with the current case. His answer was, to say the least, quite abrupt and very emphatic: "We have no reason to believe this matter is in any way connected with our inquiries and we are not going down that road."

Firmly put in our place, we quietly packed our gear and left. It would appear on the face of it, that the Cromwell Street inquiry was in no way linked with the mystery of Mary Bastholm or university student, Lucy Partington.

Mass media

As the Cromwell Street body count rose, so did the ranks of media. They arrived from London in droves, armed with cameras by the kit bag full, wearing their confidence and street-wise brashness on their sleeves. They didn't just enter the city, they invaded it. They were Everyman. Everywhere. On the streets, on the doorsteps, knocking, probing, seeking, positively finding angles new to everyone.

Each new story produces a crop of fresh sources, the very seed corn of news coverage. The local man is wise to the value of these inroads, he knows not to overstep the mark, to stay within the bounds of decency, for that's where his bread is buttered. Visiting national paper staffers with a here-today-gone-tomorrow lifestyle, are somewhat removed from these considerations. Stories, photos and deadlines are the all-important factor. They may never return and should they, it will probably be to another area, another district. They have little to lose and everything to gain by riding roughshod for a couple of days to get their words and pictures. If they have to tread on a few toes and upset a few locals, Amen. Our London colleagues brought not only their vast array of news-gathering equipment—they also brought cash.

Chequebook journalism was alive, but not very well, in Gloucester. Eager to buy up pictures and stories of anything Cromwell, they knocked doors and visited pubs in the quest.

The word was out and travelled like wildfire. The more dubious locals latched on to the pot of gold at the end of the road. Suddenly it seemed that Frederick West had worked in every house in the area. In every street in the neighbourhood. Laboured the length and breadth of Gloucester. He had built patios and extensions galore. He had restored kitchens and cellars. Dug foundations and erected walls. Wherever concrete was laid he had mixed it, poured it, shovelled it. He was, it seemed, a veritable one-man Wimpey!

A tap on the shoulder, a 'come with me' and another excited reporter exchanged 'readies' for rubbish.

They bought photographs purporting to be Fred West naked, Fred West in the midst of an orgy, Fred West at a party. One thing was sure, they were not images of Fred West. They were images that looked like Fred West. Some journalists eager to justify their expenses, their very existence, bought blind and burnt their fingers in the act

It was rumoured in Cromwell Street—the street of rumours—that one lady was better off by several hundred pounds because a photograph of her appeared in a Fleet Street tabloid, captioned as Rose West at a fancy dress party. Talk of her lucrative out-of-court settlement, unlike much of the terrace gossip, was true.

Folk with genuine stories to tell, were bought up for large sums and contracted to silence, proving that money talks. In general, our London peers are decent, down-to-earth souls. Behind all the bravado and the Anglo-Saxon expletives, they have hearts of gold and a golden lifestyle. Their expense-account living, like their alcoholic intake, was, up until the nineties, legendary. The drinking a pleasant necessity, for where else can one gain information so easily, so readily, as in the local pub. A few well-placed beers will break the ice, oil necks, start the chat. When the backslapping and bonhomie extends around the bar, the journalist, like a hovering hawk, prepares to strike. Now it's to late to be aware, be careful with words, The drink has fuddled the mind, clouded the issue.

From behind this protective haze, questions are put and answers obtained. A harvest of facts gathered in. And so it goes on, from assignment to assignment.

The need of drink to beget information. The obtaining of information begat by drink. And it works every time. These men of ink and flashbulb eat, drink and be merry, sometimes to the point of oblivion. A wise man will keep his distance from their night-time haunts, certainly if he has a limited budget and wants a clear head next day. They always alight on the best hotels and, regardless of the antics of the night before, are always ready to face whatever the next day throws at them. They even have their own language. To journalists, photographers are known as 'monkeys' or 'snappers', the cameras their 'toys'. In turn, the snappers call journalists 'blunts' (in a reference to pencils). The phone is the 'trumpet' and 'branks' is the term used by both for blank receipts. These once had a swap currency value equal to the buying power of the dollar in Eastern Europe!

There is a virtual dictionary of such terminology entitled *Monkey Speak*, brilliantly observed and documented by *Daily Mail* journalist Paul Harris. It details a language infused with Anglo-Saxon verbs and cockney rhyming slang which, out of context, appears vulgar yet strangely, when overheard, seems to melt into the general conversation causing no offence to the ear, earthy charm softening the shock of the crude. Like all big spenders, generosity is in their nature. Lend you a quid, give you their last fag, stand you a pint, even share a 'smudge' (Fleet Street slang for photograph), but en masse and in full flight they can seem as intimidating as the hordes of Ghengis Khan, and now, Gloucester was at their mercy.

For any community living under such a journalistic tornado, the pressures are enormous. Already they have experienced the local papers, regional radio and television, then coped with the national dailies, radio, television and agencies. But for a news event of such magnitude this is only the beginning, the start of a tumultuous tide that batters the senses.

The Sundays arrive in the wake of the dailies, the weeklies follow the Sundays, the monthlies next, chased by magazine colour writers, television researchers, producers of in-depth television documentaries and, in the rear, potential authors. A media mass at every door knocker, every phone, they are on each street corner, in the local shop, buying rounds in the local pubs, seeking the revealing sound bite, the shocking photo, the elusive exclusive.

Reeling from the onslaught, residents could be forgiven for thinking it will soon be over. Please, It cannot possibly continue much longer—but this is only the beginning. The are not to know that next wave will arrive with foreign accents from other lands. Name a country and they are there: German, Spanish, Italian, French, Japanese, Canadian, Swedish, Greek, Brazilian—seemingly, the whole world fetches up in Gloucester. The locals are in the eye of a storm. Leaving their homes, ferrying kids to school, doing the shopping, going to work, popping to the pub, they are sandwiched between an army of police and a let-loose media wolf pack. Under international siege.

At first it was a fascinating change from the norm, a bit of excitement, a break from the everyday, but now turned into a living hell. Householders resort to hiding behind twitching drapes, refuse to answer the urgent letterbox rattle, take the phone off the hook, turn up the volume on the TV. They retreat to the inner sanctum, seeking peace and quiet at cooker or sink. Considering the massive world-wide press presence and its ensuing overwhelming impact on the district, the occupants of Cromwell Street and St Michael's Square were amazingly compliant during the three months of sharing their environment with guests uninvited.

Eastern prayers

The police—noting we had a front seat view from the rear of properties in St Michael Square to their landscaping activities in the Wests' back yard—erected even higher screens to block our line of sight. Of course the press retaliated with a counter-offensive. A little research brought us to Mr Islam's property, an end-terrace house in St Michael's Square.

His neat-as-a-new-pin home and family were in the midst of Ramadan, the Muslim religious equivalent of Lent. The strictness of their faith meant that for a whole month, no food or liquid would pass their lips between sunrise and sunset. One could only admire their dedication, considering the mouth-watering, exotic eastern aromas that wafted from Mrs Islam's stove as she prepared the longed-for evening meal—a feast the family could only salivate over until darkness fell. Despite the lack of sustenance, Mr Islam did have something in his favour. A back garden that put us, once again, adjacent to Wests' garden.

All that was needed was the assembly of a simple scaffold platform to overcome the latest police barriers and we'd be in business again. Currying favour with both Mr Islam and cash-eager builders restoring a property two doors away, yielded a pile of bent poles, warped planks and makeshift clamps which, when cobbled together, mysteriously blossomed into a swaying temporary stage above the Islam's empty garden.

As a flock of camera-wielding starlings, we made the short flight over two backyards to the new nest. There we clung, ignorant of danger, as new angles and images were revealed to the cameras' views. This cheeky chink in the police force barricades had brought a halt to their efforts to blind our lenses. Remarkably, the platform stayed unhindered in the garden until police left 25 Cromwell Street some two months later.

The emptying

If I was not hanging around the scaffold tower, with its looming view into the back garden of Cromwell Street, I wandered the area looking for daily events at which the camera could be pointed. The occasional hint or mention from fellow journalists (and not forgetting friendly police officers) often guided me to the right place just in time. Without these helpful tips, often in code, the camera would have been blind to many of the happenings. In the teeth of a biting wind, an officer of the law murmured, as we chatted about the weather: "Yeah, it's much warmer the other side".

Knowing he was giving out clues, traipsing mud through Mrs Islam's pristine kitchen, I arrived in the nick of time to see the contents of 25 Cromwell Street being removed via the front door. Furniture, carpets, toolboxes, video players, televisions, followed by a bath complete with plumbing and literally the kitchen sink, all carried by grim-faced policemen into waiting vans. Incongruously adorning the front wall of the Wests' house was an ornate wrought iron name plate, more suitable for an up-market detached bungalow than the uninspiring semi. The elaborate metalwork words spelling '25 Cromwell Street', made by Fred West himself, had now become a world-infamous artwork. The sign was adopted by the media as a symbol for the 'House of Horrors', heading every newspaper story and television item regarding Fred and Rose West. To deter morbid memorabilia freaks stealing the sign, it too was unscrewed from the façade and taken into police custody, along with vanloads of domestic items removed from the house. A large crowd gathered to witness the bizarre proceedings.

Like extras on the set of a TV medical soap opera, the crowd regularly appeared on cue for every major operation in the street. The information grapevine never let them down. "There's his hammer", "that's his axe" were among the asides whispered from the crowd as we filmed the emptying of the forlorn charnel house.

Methodically, before their wide-eyed faces, the building was having its vital organs ripped out: drastic surgery to clear the guts of the property for further exploratory examinations, dramatic incisions, intended not to save the house, but to put it out of its misery for ever. A place that was once a home without a heart, now a testimony to death, its last signs of life ebbing away through the front door.

Artful Dodgers

The St Michael's Square builders were not the only enterprising folk who turned over a few bob amid Cromwell Street's swarm of press and people. Like a modern-day version of Brecht's 'Mother Courage', café owners and stallholders followed the media's footsteps as in the classic stage play set in Europe in 1618.

Then traders trudged behind armies to sell their food and wares, and women their bodies. Now *we* had replaced those foot soldiers (thankfully no-one was selling their body, or not to my knowledge anyway), but we were grateful for the sustenance of food and drink which fought off the winter cold.

Forever worried of missing an important event in the fast-unfolding news scenario, we dared not leave our temporary hamlet for café comfort and repast without back-up. So the streetwise, profit-hungry vendors mingling among police, press and public, offering hot drinks, pies and sandwiches, were most welcome. Previously blank windows displayed hastily-scribbled cards offering cheap accommodation, tasty snacks or comfortable rooms for the night.

Traders descended with printed tracts advertising their premises for 'good food at fair prices'. The atmosphere was that of a medieval gathering: all that was missing was a public hanging. Our days were marked by new tricks and events we could not escape.

We also became 'of the street'—accepting the strange as normal. An unfortunate inhabitant races naked along the street. There is no sense of shock from his peers. No head turning, this was their normal. Fast also becoming our normal. Another day, another sad soul ranting and raving, his screams bouncing off the red brick walls, his mind lost.

Gently but firmly he is removed from the pathetic bedsit by staff of a nearby clinic. The locals barely raise their eyebrows. More disturbing than this is the fact that we too begin to accept these abnormalities as normal. We are slowly, methodically, becoming Cromwellised. If these were bizarre days we witnessed, it was only the beginning. The surface of the story, like the house, had hardly been scratched by either police or press.

Commuting

After 35 years of never knowing from one minute to the next where I would be or what tomorrow would bring, I was actually travelling to a place of work. For the first time in three decades I had a steady job. A regular routine.

Each morning rise, swaddle myself in warm garments and motor daily with sleepy-eyed fellow travellers along the road to Gloucester. I was doing something I always said I'd never do—commuting. My travelling companions journeyed to factories, shops and office computers. Mine was a journey to crime.

On arrival, there was the luxury of three 'air-conditioned offices': the front door of Cromwell Street, the rear door of Cromwell Street and the lofty windswept platform overlooking the deathly garden plot. All three positions were within a 100-yard walk.

Days were spent roaming between each, via a rubbish-strewn alleyway and a doctors' surgery that afforded a short-cut from front to back—with camera on shoulder, pockets stuffed with spare batteries, tapes and a small 35mm camera, also used when possible to record events at Cromwell Street. Generally I had to abandon all thoughts of still photography, the TV filming being always a priority in the struggle to feed the insatiable appetite of unrelenting news bulletins. The camera rolled for the arrival of the police digging teams, their change of shifts, their going home.

Every nuance of the emerging news story was recorded. The inquiry was developing so fast and becoming so big, nothing could be left to chance. At Central TV's Gloucester dock-side offices, a large cabinet held the daily input of video tapes. These were conscientiously numbered, dated and marked with a firm 'not to leave the building' notice. As the story grew, so the tapes piled up. Within a month, over one hundred half-hour cassettes lined the cabinet, all cross referenced and filed for posterity. A digital documentation of evil.

Aggression

I spent many of the Cromwell Street days, and several nights, on my own, dwelling in that lonely no-man's land betwixt police and public, often frustrated by the former and sometimes harassed by the latter. The harassment took many forms: possibly an evil grimace, a glance accompanied with an aggressive v-sign, or a snarled "f**k off". One occasion stands out from most. Around 11.30 pm, just myself and a diminutive female police officer at the front gate of 'The House of Horrors'.

I was on the 'dark watch' from 7pm until 1am. The reason for the vigil escapes me now—an editor's whim or hunch perhaps, who's to know. It was Saturday night and the pubs were closing. A sea of black faces swam past, laughing, shouting, inquiring—all jovial, no problem. Silence resumed for a while when suddenly I was confronted by an unsmiling white man, obviously unhappy and verbally very aggressive.

I had seen him during the previous weeks as he lived directly opposite the house of Fred and Rosemary West. Now he was drunk and for some reason, I was the target of his hostility. Interpreting his alcoholic ranting, it seemed that my daytime colleagues had been instrumental in stopping him visiting his estranged wife and child. How or why, I knew not, but this was the gist of his rage.

There was no way of appeasement, I was the root of all his troubles. While he raved, I talked back. The police officer suggested he go home but he stood his ground and continued the verbal abuse. This I could take, it was the physical I was worried about.

How to deal with such wild encounters? Keep your distance, keep talking, keep 30 pounds of newsgathering glass and metal between you and a potential flying fist. Fortunately, it never came to that. Quick as he'd flared up, he calmed down, pausing only to point a cursing finger my way. If he set eyes on me next week, I was dead. I would be wasted away, I would be history. American gang-slang threats in an English street, somehow out of kilter when delivered with a Gloucester accent. Then he left, his still fury hanging on the air, his threat on hold till Monday.

The start of the week found me in back at Cromwell Street and lo, he was back there too. He moved purposely in my direction, I braced myself for another verbal onslaught. His hand came up, this time not in anger but a gesture of peace. An apology formed on his lips: "I was out of order Saturday night mate, I'm sorry, had too much to drink, trouble with the missus, OK?" He said his name was Shane. We shook hands, I mouthed the traditional "no problem", agreeing we'd have a drink one night in the local. We never did. Perhaps one day.

Acceptance

The press and police have a strange marriage of convenience. A sort of Victorian coupling, often cold but understood and tolerated by both partners. When they need us they can be almost warm and we lap it up. When they are totally in control they offer little, maybe a sardonic glance for which we have to be grateful. As in many arranged marriages, it's a very one-sided affair.

At Cromwell Street, courtesy of information from the man in the cells, they were very much in control, very much the dominant partner of this one-sided arrangement. To them, I must have been a pain in the ass. Always there, filming morning, noon and evening. At the start of each digging day alighting from their van, my winter-wrapped, swollen shape was the first thing their eyes fell on.

There again at dusk, still recording these temporary sons of the soil depart for the relief of home, a respite from the macabre demolition of an urban garden. At first they never glanced my way, gave no acknowledgement of my presence. As time passed I received the odd glance, occasional nod.

Slowly they softened, warming up—if only luke—to my persistence, maybe acknowledging my journalistic determination. The change came one bitterly cold day, a policeman leaving the caravan 'incident room' offered me coffee, for which I was very grateful. Although still not part of 'them', I was at last considered 'safe'. Now they daily greeted me by my first name and exchanged small talk. They never gave anything away, the odd thrown question would be parried with a wry smile or casual shrug. The policemen's plot remained a very private one. To me, it seemed the yawning gap between press and police had narrowed a little, yet the very nature of their task and our wants, meant it could never be fully closed, but at least it was a start.

Foreign bodies

The dozing giant of journalism in the form of the European and world press, its nose tweaked by reports from its London agents, awoke from slumber, rubbed the sleep from its eyes and headed across continents into the city of Gloucester. Causing media numbers already there to pale into insignificance.

The infiltrating mass of international newsgathers set up shop in St Michael's Square, their TV dishes sprouted like mammoth mushrooms in the car park, ready to beam words and pictures to the earth's four corners. Cromwell Street became a jumble of United Nations, a babbling mass of foreign accents, foreign folk, desperately trying to sort fact from fiction, frantically grabbing sound bites from anyone who knew Frederick West. From anyone who knew anything. From anyone.

Jet lagged and confused, they roamed the area, fighting against the clock and international time-zone deadlines. Seeing them struggle with scant knowledge of events, in alien surroundings, in some cases without fluency of the English language, one could only admire their resolve to create a logical report out of such chaos. As a respite from the daily digging scenario at Cromwell Street, I was assigned with Central TV's reporter, Clare Lafferty, to follow the 'international brigade' for an incestuous television piece regarding our foreign 'brothers'. There was not much travel involved, all we did was stand on a corner and wait for the world to pass by.

The questions put to our overseas colleagues were simple and to the point: "How is this story being received in your country?". The reporter from Australian TV stated in his rich antipodean accent: "We are fascinated, it's really big back home. This is not a few thousand hectares in the bush with bodies scattered everywhere, this is a small terraced house in an English suburb, with possibly up to twenty bodies buried in the garden. For us in Australia, this is just like Coronation Street!".

The Canadian TV team explained that their editor, reacting to the wire reports, had decided this was going to develop into a very big story, hence their arrival. No, they had never heard of Gloucester before, but it was a strange way to put it on the map!

So our morning continued, grabbing short sharp succinct pieces from Brazil, Italy, France, Spain and Germany. The beautiful reporter from a Japanese TV station, dressed in a powder blue suit and with a complexion as delicate as fine bone china, declined giving an interview as they were up against a deadline.We gracefully accepted her reason and let the camera roll anyway as she made her live presentation to the Japanese nation from the front door of the Wests' house. It turned out to be one of our best clips of the day. Checking with the producer before her piece to camera, she struggled to establish the body count and their locations within the house: "There two bodies in the kichin ... five in the baffwoom ... fwee in the gardin ... no .. fwee in the kichin ... two in the baffwoom ... four in the gardin ... or was it fwee in the gardin ... one in the baffwoon"? She let out a frustrated yell then, composed, began her report in her native language. Everything was fine until she came up against the confusing consonants in Cromwell Street and Frederick West. "Fwedwik Rest .. Fwedrik Vest". Realising her mistake she started again, leading off with: "Cwomwill Seat" then "Convall Sweet", with panic setting in she tried again. We kindly moved on to another country.

Press gang

As the Cromwell Street body count grew, the media presence in Gloucester multiplied by the day. It became clear that the police canteen would be inadequate for further press gatherings so arrangements were made to hold future press conferences in the lecture hall of the nearby Gloucester College of Art and Technology.

This willingness of today's police forces to accommodate and respond to the needs the press and media reflects how much their attitude has changed over my working life. I am reminded of one example of how it was in the 'bad old days', when as a youngster working at a Hereford picture agency, I was dispatched to an upmarket area on the edge of the town following a tip-off about police activity in the area. Armed with my boss's faithful Rolleiflex camera, I proudly set off in the office Morris Minor on my first crime story.I soon spotted a group of police officers and plain-clothed detectives huddled round a garden gate. With camera slung round my neck, I strode confidently towards them. "What you want"? demanded a hefty detective. I explained I was from the news agency and asked what was happening. His answer was a succinct: "F**k off!" Their bellowing laughter rang in my ears as I retreated with my tail between my legs. Thankfully things have moved on a great deal. All constabularies now appoint dedicated press officers to handle the media's requests for information, interviews and photo opportunities. The police have come to recognise the real value that the media can bring to their investigations. Since the early 1960s, Gloucestershire Constabulary has appointed many officers from the ranks to act as press officers—police officers first, press officers second. But for all that, they accepted the posting and many came to enjoy their friendly cat-and-mouse role with members of the press.

Among the more recent were Mike Humphries, Jack Cratchley, David Morgan and Colin Handy. Morgan and Handy were heavily involved, and very helpful to the media, during the Cromwell Street enquiry. Working alongside them and heading the press office team was former journalist Hilary Allison, the first civilian press officer to be appointed by Gloucestershire Constabulary as well as the first woman in that particularly hot seat. A tall and striking woman, Hilary took the constant bombardment of media questions in her stride, always with a smile and never becoming flustered or impatient.She quickly won over the 'fourth estate' to become favourite of the media gang, and was dubbed 'the angel of Cromwell Street'. While this pet name probably first came about because of her attractive and friendly way of dealing with the press, Hilary didn't just pass on official facts. Not infrequently, she found herself the focus of press comments during the enquiry. The *Western Daily Press* described her as: ".. taming the tabloid terrors—the small still voice of reason." The *Daily Express* wrote: "She has earned the affectionate nickname with her calm approachable manner." The

Gloucestershire Echo described her as: "..an angel amid the horror of Cromwell Street." *The Times* mentioned her as being: "..helpful, efficient and patient—characteristics entirely absent in many of her counterparts on other forces." When the Cromwell Street saga came to its eventual end, Hilary flapped her angel wings and took off to a new post with Thames Valley police. By then, her unlooked-for fame had been transformed into 'police speak'. Now colleagues in other forces were being asked by their seniors to 'do a Hilary'. At first baffled, they soon learned that this translated into handling a media interview or police press announcement. The expression 'to do a Hilary' has now entered the annals of police life.

On Monday March 28th the media shambled into the college grounds. The huge room set aside for the event was solid with the cream of British and international journalism. A wash of floodlights rained down on the hastily arranged top table, at which were seated John Bennett, his number two Terry Moore and Gloucestershire police press officers Colin Handy, Hilary Allison and David Morgan. These formal gatherings of press and police were not only stunning in their magnitude but electrifying in their revelations. The solemn police team faced a mass of step ladders supporting rows of wobbling photographers, all amid ranks of reporters, pens poised over virgin notebooks in expectation of ever more gruesome facts.

By now nine bodies had been unearthed from inside the house and garden at Cromwell Street but so far only three had been named. Fred and Rose's daughter, Heather West, Shirley Robinson and Carol Cooper. Now other names were to be revealed. Detective Superintendent John Bennett, addressing the impatient media scrum, remained unflustered. Projecting his words in their warm Gloucestershire burr to the very back of the hall: "Ladies and gentlemen, I will read a statement regarding police investigations at Cromwell Street and situation to date. There will be no questions. Copies of this statement will be available and I will do one-to-one readings for television and radio stations at the end of proceedings. But I repeat, there will be no questions taken or answered today".

With cameras rolling on his every utterance, he paused to draw breath, then revealed the names of four more victims.

A silence hung over the hall as he announced: "18-year-old Juanita Mott ... 19-year-old Linda Gough ...17-year-old Alison Chambers" ... and finally ... "21-year-old Lucy Partington".

The shocking discovery of Lucy's remains closed the book on a Cheltenham mystery that had been in police records and local journalists' minds since December 1973. I had covered the news of her disappearance at the time, providing Fleet Street with pictures of the missing student as well as filming the various intense police probes that took place throughout the county. 21-year-old Lucy, a third-year student studying English at Exeter University, was in Gloucestershire staying with her mother over the Christmas festivities. On the evening of Thursday December 27th, Lucy visited a friend's home in the Pittville area of Cheltenham. After a pleasant social evening, during which she drafted a letter of application for a post-graduate position in London, she waved her goodbyes and was last seen rushing off to catch the post box, before taking the bus back to her mother in Gretton, a village some eight miles away. Luck was not with Lucy that night. She never returned to the home and Christmas hearth of her family.

As the local freelance, it was natural I became quite involved in the case, even at one point driving Lucy's mother to ATV's studios in Birmingham. There she made an impassioned appeal on the evening programme for her daughter to get in touch if she had any problems, pleading also if anyone knew of her whereabouts to make contact with her or the police.

The journey to the midlands was undertaken with a strange mixture of compassion and strained casualness, conversation stilted, hesitant as we stayed off painful subjects. Mrs Partington, an architect by profession, bravely undertook the task, facing up to the cameras without any outward sign of nerves. Not easy to do in normal situations let alone in such heart-rending circumstances. With the TV interview over, we made an almost wordless journey back to the sadness of her Cotswold home. With an uncanny similarity to the disappearance of Mary Bastholm five years earlier, Lucy had innocently waited to catch a bus. Mary had waited in the cold of January, Lucy waited in the chill December. Like Mary, she never climbed aboard her bus. She just vanished.

Over two decades later, Cromwell Street had given up Lucy's pitiable remains. Was it possible that the other mystery remaining on Gloucester police files, the whereabouts of Mary Bastholm, would also be resolved in the same tragic way? One thing was certain, Mary would not be found at 25 Cromwell Street—she went missing long before Frederick and Rosemary West moved into the dismal Victorian property.

Rumours

Fred West's flamboyant solicitor, Howard Ogden (his business card displayed the slogan: 'If you're nicked phone Oggi'), decided in the midst of the police 'pressers' to call a conference of his own to counteract the growing unrestrained media coverage with its stamp of 'penny dreadful' headlines.

He was angered by the tabloid interpretation of events he considered to be unfair to his client, who was still innocent in the eyes of the law. He invited the press to coffee and biscuits at Cheltenham's Golden Valley Hotel and proceeded to admonish the assembly for their lack of responsible reporting.

They drank the coffee, scoffed the biscuits, recorded verbatim his chiding speech then, totally unrepentant, removed to the hotel bar for the respite of a liquid lunch. Back at Cromwell Street, with Ogden's remonstrations a thing of the past, they sought new angles and fresh revelations in their accustomed manner. In reality there was no stopping them, the 'House of Horrors' was the journalistic centre of the universe, Cromwell Street the fount of all rumours.

The exclusives continued hitting the headlines. The *Sunday Mirror* was prolific, they had everyone running in circles. Each week they came out with new disclosures of evil that rocked the city. 'Possibly twenty Cromwell Street victims exclusive'. 'House of Horrors victims decapitated exclusive'. And so it went on, facts mixed with rumours. Rumours becoming facts.

Since the early days, we had heard these tales rumbling around the terraced streets. Limbs missing, heads bound with masking tape, digits unaccounted for—the rumours persisted. Grew large.

'West had confessed to twenty-five murders'. Even the number of his home in Cromwell Street and his former homes in Midland Road and Bishop's Cleeve, took on a macabre satanic significance. All were numbered twenty-five. It became a cult figure. Some locals were convinced it was no coincidence. The number twenty-five was symbolic of Fred's sins. He had killed twenty-five people. Double it, There could be fifty victims! When did he start? Where did he stop? Add all the numbers up, he might have done to death seventy-five! These wild witchcraft interpretations surfaced daily throughout the labyrinth of roads that made up the district where the Wests lived. Like all rumours, we treated them with disdain, a pinch of salt, yet reminded ourselves, no smoke without fire, before filing them away in our minds.

As the *Sunday Mirror* each week revealed the terrors contained within the house, we could only surmise they had a fantastic source via the ranks of the police. How else could they have such confidence in presenting sordid details as fact. There had to be an inside man and if not now, he surely once wore a blue uniform.

Or go mad

He first became known to the world at large when brought before Gloucester magistrates' court on February 1994, as Frederick Walter Stephen West. This was the official listing of the man who would eventually be charged with the murder of twelve females. Frederick Walter Stephen West. The name destined to appear in the annals of crime alongside Jack the Ripper, Bodkin Adams, John Christie, Ian Brady and Peter Sutcliffe.

As the police support team shovelled, sieved and sorted every ounce of earth in the Cromwell Street garden, the police called another crowded press conference and the tabloids broadcast every gruesome find, Frederick Walter Stephen West was the name on the tip of everyone's tongue. After weeks of probing, chatting with his friends, his acquaintances, listening to neighbours' gossip, fact and fiction, we came to know, but never understand, Frederick Walter Stephen West.

Familiarity they say, breeds contempt. It can also, even in the most macabre of situations, create strange bedfellows. Those of us covering the daily events became very familiar.

The man languishing in Gloucester's police station cells, his fate in the lap of the gods, entered our psyche—to all of us, police, press, publicans, public—he became, Fred. Despite his alleged crimes, the evil doings, the fear, the dread instilled in the victims, the pain, the grief being shouldered by devastated relatives, he still came to be known and described colloquially, by all and sundry, as Fred.

Why? Why when referred to, was there no hint of hate in the voice? How could he be talked about as if a next-door pal, a workmate, a drinking companion, with no disgusted tone on the tongue? Perhaps because the evil he was charged with was so dreadful, so awful, we could only live with it by acknowledging the accused. Police officers on duty talked of Fred. Reporters over a pint chatted about Fred. The man in the street referred to Fred. He seemed, when discussed, a mate, a colleague, a friendly neighbour. To the ravaged families of the deceased he was evil personified. But to the world at large outside the pain and sorrow, he was Fred.

It was not long before the street was buzzing with sick jokes, the sort that always arise in the wake of terrible events. Who knows who devises them, they seem to drift in on the air. Pressure-release valves perhaps, for mere mortals, unable to cope with the vileness in their midst. Bad taste certainly, without question unforgivable, but how do undertakers, policemen, firemen, ambulance men, doctors even, cope when steeped daily in death and horror? They coin dark humour and wear black cloaks of mirth to get through the day, or otherwise go mad.

The little boys' room

Gloucester magistrates' court and police station are sandwiched between the historic cathedral and the city's ancient prison.

It was here that Fred and Rose West were brought before magistrates while on remand. As with Cromwell Street, the court became the focus of media attention and a continuing headache for the police. Siege conditions were the order of the day for the boys in blue each time the couple were brought before the bench. Having witnessed the press dodges at Cromwell Street, they were forewarned so barricades went up. The once see-through, ever-open iron gates leading to the police yard and side door of the court, were sealed shut and, for good measure, filled in with sheet metal and painted bobby-blue. Access to the police yard was altered to allow vehicles conveying prisoners to enter the yard via a pair of solid steel doors. These were remote-controlled to open or close by a given signal from the yard, and monitored by video cameras. The police station cells were originally constructed to keep felons in but now the cop shop and its yard were adapted to also keep cameras out. For the first of the Wests' husband-and-wife remand appearances in a courtroom that normally handled petty crime. I teamed up with two other TV crews. We agreed to take up different positions and share any images we obtained of the infamous couple. Now, in view of the barricades before us, it seemed a futile task.

The back walls of the police station were festooned with rows of rickety step ladders, to the top of which optimistic snappers clung for the arrival of the notorious passengers. The cavalcade, blue lights flashing, swept through the pre-arranged open doors and into the sanctuary of the protected yard. With unbelievable timing, an oil tanker arrived to deliver winter fuel to the court, parking up against the police yard in a very photogenic position. The metal ladder on the oil-smeared vehicle was irresistible. Shouting to the driver to "hang on", I slithered up its greasy rungs and by sheer luck obtained an image of Rose West as she was led into court —it wasn't great footage, but better than nothing. Five seconds of Rose West's face for that evening's news.

Needed back at Cromwell Street, I missed the next remand date photo-scrummage, and it was on this occasion the press swooped and scored. Having spotted windows in a library building overlooking the police yard, they managed to secrete themselves there and, waiting with the patience of hawks, got their reward. Pictures that winged around the world.

The first photos of Fred West since his arrest, smiling and joking with his jailers as he was led from court it, mocked everyone and said everything. The police were angry, not so much over the obtaining of the picture, that was fair game. It was Fred West's sniggering face that upset the detectives, which they rightly considered was abhorrent to the families of the dead and missing. From the outset, Detective Superintendent Bennett, was mindful of family feelings, respectful of the trauma they were facing, this was always foremost in his thinking at every press conference and off-the-cuff briefing. He was determined to do everything possible to protect them, knowing, as he did, that when the full facts were finally revealed, their pain would be unbearable. One can understand his anxiety, it was part of his job to show compassion, attempt to soften the shock. Telling the story of the unfolding events was the media's role. While the police tried to close every loophole, the press and television redoubled their efforts to find a chink in the armour.

With this in mind, it was suggested there may be a viewpoint from within the labyrinth of rooms in the Shire Hall building that towered over the police station complex. I was asked to check it out. Donning, unusually, a suit and with a slim leather brief case, I took on the mantle of office worker and roamed unheeded round the cavernous building to pinpoint possible photographic positions.

There were good views into the police yard from the landings, but no privacy. Great views from certain offices but with the problem that they were full of folk. Eventually I found what was needed—in a gentlemen's cloakroom. From the row of windows over the washbasins, all of which opened, it was possible to take in the whole of the police quadrangle. The only other item required on the chosen day would be luck. The plan went into action on the morning of the Wests' next court appearance.

I was to enter Shire Hall at its furthest point from the cloakroom and make my way, via the rambling corridors, with a dismantled video camera stored in a canvas sports bag.

Central TV's reporter, Ken Goodwin, would be outside feeding me arrival news via mobile phone—all I had to do was get past the building's security man and sit tight in the loo! Ken, employing his wicked lavatorial humour, christened me with the call sign, 'Vindaloo one'. He was to be known as 'Vindaloo two'. I once again made the journey unchallenged, entered the cloakroom unhindered and sat in one of the closets. So far so good. Now, sitting on the loo with the re-assembled camera on my lap, all one could was wait.

From time to time ablution sounds rose from the cloakroom. I prayed the mobile wouldn't ring during these occasional visits. Eventually the call came, "Vindaloo one—the van is here".

I shot out of closet, camera rolling, aimed through the pre-opened window, getting a profile shot of Rose West as she was led from the vehicle, before retreating to the sanctuary of the now-warm seat. Five minutes later the phone warbled again: "Vindaloo one. Van two has arrived". At that moment the cloakroom door opened, another bloody visitor, what are these folk on—senna pods?

Debating whether to sit tight or blow my cover, I realised there was no choice. I shot from the cubicle to find a young member of staff at the washbasin. Again filming through the window I whispered an aside: "You haven't seen me —I'm not here—OK".

His shock at seeing a man wielding a full-blown TV camera within the confines of a gent's lavatory rendered him speechless. Without drying his hands, he nodded and made a rapid exit. At the window I glimpsed a man I assumed to be Fred West, being taken out from the far side of the van and totally obscured from the lens. You win some, you lose some.

Having achieved some success, the exercise was to be repeated on the next remand date, when again I was snugly seated in the loo waiting the phone call.

When it came, once again I leapt out of the closet, this time putting the fear of God into an ITN cameraman, who having also sussed out the viewpoint, had sneaked in convinced he was on his own. "Jesus Christ, you frightened me to death" he yelled. Now sharing the view, both optically and with optimism, we trained our lenses onto the scene in the police yard.

Before either of us could fire up our videos, the door burst open and a beefy security guard told us to leave. With cameras still trained below and rolling, we spoke into the air, requested he look away, maybe come back later if he didn't mind. He stood his ground. "The police have seen you. Leave or face arrest!". "What for—going to the lav? Give us a break". All these pleas as theatrical asides, while still keeping our eyes and lenses firmly trained on the job in hand. But there was no sign below of the Wests being led into court. They were being kept in the vehicles till we were sorted out. With the security man getting more agitated and us mumbling words to the effect that we'd been thrown out of better bogs than this, we made our excuses and left.

Black looks

Authors of crime fiction often promote the theory that the villain always returns to the crime scene. True or false, had they written such a chapter regarding the Wests' murders, it would certainly have been true. Fred West was to return to four locations, admittedly courtesy of the police rather than choice, but it got him out of the cells for while.

Detectives hoped his visits might help reveal the sites of his victims, hence Cromwell Street was his first taste of fresh air, but it didn't end there. He found himself out again on the 20th March, making a visit to his former home at 25 Midland Road, just a few hundred yards from Cromwell Street. The sombre three-storey Victorian pile that looked onto Gloucester Park, over the years had been drawn and quartered into flats and bedsits. Again Fred West arrived in darkness, out of sight from prying eyes. It was decided his return would aid his tangled memory into narrowing the search for a child, his child, Charmaine, who vanished without trace in 1971.

West's two other nocturnal outings were to the Much Marcle fields during the search for his wife, Catherine Costello, and Ann McFall. His confused finger-pointing did little to assist the search; it was more of a hindrance. With Cromwell Street on the point of being sealed up, its windows blinded with steel shutters, its doors jammed with concrete, creating an unconsecrated, unoccupied mausoleum, it was getting time to move on.

Tipped off that on Wednesday April 26th, police would move to Midland Road, I mentioned this to Central TV staff but they dismissed the idea, expecting that it would be many days, maybe weeks, before the house became another search scene. Still believing my tip-off, I made for Midland Road early that spring morning, finding police already there, and also cameraman Les Leach from BBC. I wondered if he also had the same contact as me? Half an hour later we both filmed a Portakabin being sited at the back of 25 Midland Road and pictured police moving into their new home on this—day 56—of the ongoing inquiry. That morning's activities made lead stories for the day's bulletins.

Just being there had again paid off as the story entered a new phase in its bizarre telling. The unfortunate tenant of the flat where the Wests once lived, could be seen removing his furniture and belongings to make way for fresh occupants. These would turn out to be temporary, blue-overalled dwellers, guaranteed not to keep the place clean and tidy as he had, but piece by piece to take apart all with the owner's reluctant blessing.

We filmed his leaving and the removal of belongings from his home. Black looks, in the real sense, were cast our way as the gentleman of African descent, aided by friends, bore his worldly possessions out of premises which, within a month, were deemed to be tarnished by the discovery of another victim. Confronted with a new location, we negotiated with tenants for camera positions. Primed with tales of big fees paid at Cromwell Street, they asked silly money and got nothing. Next door to the now empty flat lived Heather, her husband Dave and a big German Shepherd dog. The couple were very accommodating, offering a lean-to conservatory with out-of-the-weather views to the back garden. With promise of tea and rolls thrown in for good measure, we struck a deal, planning also to keep the dog happy with Alsatian-size titbits—a small price to pay against being savaged. We had a mirror image of the Cromwell Street probe but now in comfort, as spades flashed in the spring sunlight and earth-filled wheelbarrows trundled to the sieve-sorting teams in this mother of all riddles.

As the days went by we sometimes heard the cry: "Where's our doughnuts?" or "Bring on the chelseas" rising over the squeaking wheelbarrows and shovelled earth. The diggers at Midland Road were a new team comprised from the police support group and I suddenly twigged what the fuss was about. During the weeks prior, having been 'accepted' by the team in the Wests' garden, I had made a small gesture of two dozen doughnuts for the lads. This must have been mentioned at the time back at HQ, hence the now gentle heckling. The next day to muted cheers, I handed the team a fresh bag of buns and their nagging ceased. While the garden was turned over as freshly as a spring allotment, the house echoed to the sound of internal searchings and reverberated to the cacophony of drills and jackhammers cutting through the interior. The building's cellar was opened to daylight with yawning gaps appearing in its exterior walls. Mask-faced, brick-framed officers could be seen excavating amid the dust and gloom of the eerie basement, methodically disembowelling the house.

After nine days of pickaxe, chisel, sledgehammer and sieve, on Wednesday May 4th the skeleton of eight-year-old Charmaine West was revealed. For near on a quarter of a century she had lain eight feet below the footsteps of various other residents innocently going about their domestic chores. As headlines became emblazoned with the latest grim find, the next-named victim, other folk out there, anxious for missing loved ones, could be forgiven for heaving heartfelt sighs of relief. No news might be good news.

At 25 Cromwell Street and 25 Midland Road, the police teams were thorough, precision-like, in the hunt for victims of Fred and Rose West. They had to be. They were talking to a madman, discussing with a demon, obtaining information from a liar. His story changed, his deeds altered at each inquisition. If he said there were only two bodies, it was possible there were more. When he stated categorically there were more, there could be none. At times he was a self-declared serial killer, on other occasions he claimed total innocence.

Rose West as always, answered: "I'm innocent" to each charge put to her—or remained cell-silent. With West hinting at others unknown and unnamed, confronted with such mind-blowing facts and fictions, the police had only one option, leave no stone unturned. Check every inch of every building. They probed the obvious, inspected the unconsidered, followed up the unbelievable. Doing so prolonged the inquiry, searching where they didn't want to, as well as where they knew they must. After the finding of Charmaine's remains, they continued the search at Midland Road relentlessly. It would take another three weeks before confirmation that there were no other human remains in, or under, the flat.

Charmaine was the only mortal recovered from 25 Midland Road. There was no company in death for Catherine Costello's child—she lay alone in her grave of gravel.

Cider country

Gloucestershire's hard-pressed police force had so far managed to cope with press, public and weather during the series of investigations into the so-called 'House of Horrors'. They had contained the media at Cromwell Street and the magistrates' court and during the search and digging at Midland Road. It was on their western flank, a county away, that they faced an uphill struggle. During the hours of questioning Fred West regarding the whereabouts of his first wife, Catherine, and their friend Ann McFall, his tangled mind managed to come up with a couple of places in rural Herefordshire. These revelations led police to feel more confident they would solve the mystery disappearance of his wife and the young teenager. The locations he pinpointed were known as Letterbox Field and Fingerpost Field.

Both sites were only a mile or so from Fred's childhood home at Much Marcle. The village, a pretty rural backwater famed for the cider-making skills of the dynastic Weston family, was now destined for a different sort of fame, thanks to the black arts of one of its sons.

On Saturday March 5th in the company of detectives, West was driven to Letterbox Field, where he attempted to guide officers to the grave of Catherine. Aided only by the diminishing memory of the accused, the small group walked the land as West suggested, and pointed out various areas where Catherine could, or might be. Either he was conning them or he genuinely forgot, one will never know.

A little frustrated, the police returned their prisoner to his Gloucester cell, hoping his memory would improve. The following Monday, West returned to the area, this time visiting Fingerpost Field, hopefully to aid detectives establish the site of Ann McFall's burial place. The outcome for the police was much the same at the previous Saturday. Fred West walked around kicking the earth, admitted he knew her but was not her killer. He then helpfully indicated alternative spots where he thought her remains might be. He could not explain how he knew this, or how she came to meet her death! After this bizarre outing he was again put back in his cell.

Frustratingly for the police, amid all the acres of land before them, they had still not been able to pinpoint the sites of Catherine's or Ann's burials.

Fred West had married Catherine in November 1962 in the Herefordshire market town of Ledbury. Not long after the wedding, Fred and his wife moved north, settling in Glasgow where, in May 1963 and July 1964, their two children Charmaine and Anne-Marie, were born. The couple had befriended a young girl named Ann McFall who eventually moved in with the Wests, helping out as babysitter and nanny to the children. When the Wests decided, in

1966, to return to Gloucestershire, the Glaswegian teenager, now very much part of the family, moved south with them. An adventure for a young girl that should have been filled with hope and excitement, it was to become a journey from which no traveller returns.

Twenty-five years on, in the April of 1994, at the outset of the body searches in Letterbox Field and Fingerpost Field, police and others involved did not believe Fred West could have forgotten the whereabouts of his victims' graves.

How could he forget something so terrible? Would you? Yet landscapes alter, recognisable marker hedges get grubbed out, age and wind demolish signpost trees. The earth moves. Without the familiar landmarks to prompt memories, no matter how horrific, it is possible over the passage of decades to completely forget—or more likely not want to remember, or even more likely to give the 'Old Bill' the runaround.

Whatever the truth, somewhere in those fertile growing fields, Fred had buried two people—first his wife, then on another occasion, young Ann McFall. He had scooped two graves from the red rich Hereford soil, within which to hide his vileness. The undulating pastoral scene with the toytown names of Fingerpost Field and Letterbox Field would eventually yield their bones. But only with a struggle. West had given names to the locations but that was all.

In the real sense of the phrase, he had lost the plot. On March 29th, a team of twelve police diggers moved onto Letterbox Field to start the grisly hunt for Catherine West.

Confronted with acres of windswept land during their rain-soaked soil search, they could not have known that nearly three months later, bathed in warm sunshine, they would still be combing the surrounding land. Still searching the killing fields of rural Herefordshire. After nine days' digging, things were not going well at Letterbox Field. The climate and the sodden earth, combined with the fact they were working without accurate site-digging pointers, literally shovelling in the dark, brought each day's end to a negative result. So once again on April 6th, Fred West walked the land. Maybe this time he told the truth or maybe the police just got lucky. Five days after his visit, Letterbox Field gave up its secret. At noon Sunday April 10th, only a few yards into the field from the tarmac highway to Much Marcle, human bones were discovered. These were later confirmed as being the remains of Catherine West.

Now the police could close the gate on the acres at Letterbox and focus their efforts on the neighbouring field to seek the whereabouts of Ann McFall. Throughout the whole rural search phase, the gods threw every sort of weather at them—sleet, snow, frost, howling wind, torrential downpours and the gladly-welcomed sun.

As the snows melted, the spring warmth turned the soil into a vast quagmire, confronting detectives and diggers alike with a near impossible task. Only when the mud dried out was the team able to handle the land again. Their earth-moving created an immense swimming pool-sized crater, 100ft x 60ft and 8ft deep, carving an ugly scar across the once postcard-pretty landscape.

They lifted, sifted, sorted, 2,800 tonnes of soil. Each wheelbarrowof excavated earth was tipped onto a conveyor belt feeding the soil to a marquee, affording the sifters and sorters cover and privacy from peeping eyes. Painstakingly every clod, each lump of blush-red earth was hand-checked for clues, man-checked for signs of humanity.

Gloucestershire police force almost created their own financial grave in the search for the two women. It became the longest police excavation in British history, finally coming to a close on June 7th when they found what they were seeking in Letterbox Field. After days, weeks and months of spade work the soil finally gave up the body of the missing teenage girl from Scotland. When police gave the farmer his fields back, crops were already shooting through the soil, searching for the summer sun.

Cops and robbers

During his time in custody Fred West was questioned on 151 occasions, the head-aching interviews stretching over a total of 110 hours, as detectives battled to unravel his warped mind and sort truth from lies.

As he confessed, within the confines of his temporary cell, to monstrous deeds, the police could do little but act on them, extending their parameters beyond the pale, beyond belief. In the midst of mounting facts and locations, the police still had to deal with their day-to-day work, keeping on top of petty crooks who, if not held in check, would have a field day, a veritable criminal bonanza.

The 250 uniformed and plain-clothed officers of the Gloucester Division (within whose command fell Cromwell Street and Midland Road) served a population of 135,000 people. Such folk who, in the fifteen months from January 1994 to March 1995, made 86,000 personal visits or phone calls to the Division. Officers dealt with 26,500 reported crimes, arrested 7,900 people and attended 1,450 road accidents.

These statistics are the everyday incidents, logged in the normal course of duty dealing with theft, robbery, fisticuffs, accidents, muggings and lost children. The very stuff of a policeman's bag. As if this were not enough to keep them busy-bobbying, the 24th February 1994 presented them with total overload.

A report of a body in a garden. A probable wild-goose chase, local gossip exaggerated by hearsay, nevertheless something that would have to be checked out. They were not to know then that they were taking the initial steps over a terrain of terror.

Ghouls

Gloucester was no doubt besmirched by the alleged doings of its now most infamous inhabitant. Unheard of, and unknown in many parts of the world, the city was suddenly a household name in such far-flung locations as Tokyo, Alaska and Brazil. Such a world-wide reputation could have been a tourist officer's dream but, of course, foreigners were making their way to the county and city for the wrong reasons. They diverted from Stratford and Bath, travelled from Broadway and Bourton, not to admire the cathedral or the medieval buildings, nor to soak up the county's history. They cared little about Dick Whittington, the founder of Sunday Schools, Robert Raikes, or the wanton deeds of Oliver Cromwell.

The only Cromwell they wanted to know about was Cromwell Street. German, French, Dutch and Japanese tourists adjusted their itineraries so as to take in the once-home of the West family. They poured into the cramped street and ogled at press, police and locals.

They verbally prodded guarding policemen with questions, recorded the house on video and Canon sure-shot cameras and posed in front of the charnel house while friends immortalised them on film. And it wasn't just overseas visitors: folk from Birmingham, London and Plymouth fetched up in the area too, cruising the road in cars loaded with granny and kids, staring through streaky windscreen. Makes a change from Alton Towers!

One family, not content with the front view of the Cromwell Street property, made their way to the rear, struggled past abandoned household rubbish and clambered into the graveyard garden. The man, camera to hand, pictured his posing wife and child, She repeated the exercise with him and baby, creating cosy family album snaps in a backyard of hell. Next came the spoon. The man lifted several scoops of dark garden earth into a plastic shopping bag and returned from whence he came—macabreville. This weird event was witnessed by a retired gent known as Charlie, a cheerful green-fingered old boy who lived two doors from the Wests' house.

Charlie's horticultural interests kept him in the garden most days so he missed little of the happenings in Cromwell Street—and told me most. The roles were now becoming reversed. The visitors were becoming the ghouls, the press the nice guys. The locals were now witnessing another side of human nature. The stand-and-stare, gawping, intrusive brazen cheek. At least we were doing a job, there was some justification for our presence, however weak the moral argument. The inhabitants could just about cope with the vulture-like press. But these visitors were another breed, buses and carloads of human jackals, fast becoming despised creatures in the neighbourhood.

Blame

During these crazy days, the *Sunday Times* hit the streets with a devastating article on Gloucester that rocked the city fathers and insulted the townsfolk. The general tenor of the piece was that the city was populated with morons, skulking yobs roamed the streets and the place was without culture or class. Was it so surprising, therefore, that from such a community, someone like Fred West should surface?

The article was grossly disparaging to the people of Gloucester. Local newsagents, incensed by the story, reacted by burning copies of the *Sunday Times* and refusing to stock any of the Murdoch titles. An understandable, but futile, gesture as they were soon forced to selling all papers or risk receiving no supplies at all. To be sure, there is a yob culture in the city but sadly that is now common in most English towns. Considering the ethnic mix of West Indian and Asian peoples within the indigenous population, Gloucester has remained a beacon of peace compared, say, to Handsworth, Toxteth and

Bristol's St Paul's. No, the *Sunday Times* with its here today, gone tomorrow, cursory look at Gloucester, got it wrong and the writer missed out a fundamentally important point. It was in Herefordshire that Fred West was born and brought up. If it had to be necessary for some place to shoulder the guilt for such a monstrous aberration of humanity, it is my home county that needs to bear that yoke of shame, not Gloucester.

Black boxes

Of all the events in Cromwell Street during 1994, one of the most surreal took place on a pleasant, sun-filled afternoon. The word had gone round that there was to be a major happening after lunchtime. Needless to say, the press began to swarm. We waited with impatient expectation. Just after 2pm the Home Office pathologist, Professor Bernard Knight, was escorted by police officers from the side entrance of the next door house to number 25. In answer to calls from the media to pose for photographs, he stood theatrically on the doorstep of the Wests' home before disappearing through the portal.

The press were soon to discover the reason they were gathered. It was announced by the police press officer that the recovered remains of the nine victims would be shortly brought from the building and taken to Professor Knight's main laboratories at Cardiff for further analysis. A respectful silence fell over the scene as a blue-overalled member of the digging team emerged from the front door carrying a two foot square container shrouded in a black cloth.

The box and its grim contents were placed in a waiting vehicle and the officer returned indoors. This solemn little ceremony was repeated eight times more—once for each of the nine victims recovered from the house and garden.

That the occasion had been orchestrated for the media there was little doubt. In the circumstances, the police could be forgiven a certain amount of stage-management. After all, it was paramount to keep the public and press interest alerted to events— every newspaper column inch, every television newsreel might jog a memory and render new leads. The police knew the value of the press, even if they were a pain in the butt. Inside the now-gutted house, the police team who over the past two months had unrelentingly searched and retrieved Fred and Rose West's victims from the garden, interior rooms and dank cellars, decided to drawn lots to choose which of their group would carry the remains from the 'House of Horrors', who would respectfully conduct the ceremony before the silent onlooking crowds and cameras. The occasion certainly created dramatic images, photographs that found front page in next day's papers.

For television, the whole episode unfortunately appeared slightly surreal. The problem lay in using the same officer on each occasion to carry the remains from the house. When edited the images appeared as a series of jump-cuts, giving a cartoon-like effect to the material. In such sad and grave circumstances, the film item was unusable in its entirety. Hence television viewers that night saw only one set of remains being taken from the house, whichever poor soul that may have been.

Damaged

Barbara Jones lived in a flat in the Hester's Way district of Cheltenham, her address discovered in the way that journalists do, hence the arrival of Central TV's reporter Richard Barnett and me on her doorstep. Her home was in some disarray, being in the throes of decorating, but she invited us in. Her story was pathetically similar to those of so many of the young women who had entered the front door of 25 Cromwell Street. Now in her thirties, Barbara told of when, as a young teenager, she had fallen out with her parents and walked out of home.

With the arrogance of youth, she believed she could fend for herself, did not need the nagging rows that come with growing sexual awareness and teenage rebellion. Like all young who flee the nest, the real world is never as romantic as portrayed in books and films. The gloss becomes more dull with each dawning day when faced with reality. Barbara Jones eventually fetched up in Gloucester, seated on a wall in Cromwell Street—a wall right opposite the home of Fred and Rose West—worried, lonely and frightened.

A stocky, curly-headed man approached, inquiring why she was so upset. He offered help, offered sanctuary. Barbara gratefully accepted the kind invitation of hospitality. She entered the house, like so many others, innocent of the bestiality practised within its walls. If she was to be believed, and there was no reason to think otherwise, nothing untoward happened during her stay at the Wests' home. She had a room and was given meals, in return for which she babysat and generally helped about the house. She said she was never propositioned, never sexually abused, never knew of any underhand deeds at Cromwell Street.

Was she telling the truth, or could she not find the words to describe openly in front of two men, her experience of times at the Wests' home? But it was Barbara's last sentence of the interview that was so poignant. With eyes focused past the camera lens, as if not wanting to conjure faded memories, talking in a monotone voice, she spoke words that meant little, but spoke volumes: "I was one of the lucky ones, I escaped from Cromwell Street".

Was she speaking the truth or was she also tarnished for ever by the goings-on in that house? We returned some weeks later to obtain an interview for another television station. The front door of the maisonette was shattered and hanging from its hinges. The property was empty, neglected, deserted as if left in haste. Barbara had abandoned the apartment where only a short time ago she been fondly creating a home. The damaged portal a testimony to a soul in turmoil.

An interesting job

As I write this chapter I am in my seventy-sixth year. More than five decades of my life have been devoted to the chasing of news stories throughout the UK and overseas.

When asked what I do for a living, the response is always the same: "You must have a very interesting job". Confronted, camera-laden, on some assignment or other, again the same comment: 'You must have an interesting job'. If only a pound note for every one of them. Yet they are correct. It is a fascinating trade. To be first on the scene. To be at the beginning. Being paid for being nosy? Earning a living by being the eyes and ears of the people, an audience insatiable in its appetite for news. It's impossible to become bored for no two days are ever the same.

Sure there are the run-of-the-mill stories that have to be covered, the very stuff of journalistic life— Christmas, New Year births, court cases, council meetings, crashes, fires, abandoned babies and the weather, always the weather. But there is also the unexpected, the unusual, the something just around the corner. A phone call that finds you two days later in Bosnia.

The fax message that eventually, and magically, lands you in Africa. It's this fact alone that makes the work so addictive. Many of my colleagues have left newspapers, lured by lucrative offers in the public relations field. Speak to many and they regret the move. They have tasted the good life, raised their lifestyle to match the fatter bank balance and can't afford to go back. They are lost in a world of smart suits, working lunches, press releases and incestuous backslapping. Given an equal financial incentive, they would return in droves, glad to be back on the exciting front line of newsgathering. And when the unexpected arrives, the adrenalin *really* flows.

The unexpected turned up for me during a lull in the Cromwell Street proceedings. I was pulled away for an unrelated item needed for the evening programme. A parish pump row over an unsafe road. In conversation with a woman involved in the story, the proverbial statement was made: "You must have an interesting job". She inquired what else I was working on, so naturally I mentioned the 'House of Horrors' investigation.

At first there was silence from her, then to my amazement she exclaimed that she had known Fred West when she was a young girl—had babysat for him and his first wife Catherine, in their caravan home at Bishop's Cleeve, near Cheltenham. Reporters were falling over themselves to get first-hand accounts of the early days of Fred and Catherine and by sheer chance, one landed in my lap.

This exciting new lead began to evaporate as the woman explained she had only accompanied a friend on two occasions. She didn't wish to be interviewed but her once-teenage pal knew much more and would certainly be worth contacting. The next day she let me have the number of her friend, by then living near Blackpool. Later I rang and was pleasantly received by the woman, who was happy to chat openly and easily to me about her experiences. She recalled babysitting nights in the mobile home, how she befriended Fred and Catherine and came know them well and related an occasion when they offered her an album to look through.

Innocently, she had flipped the pages of what she thought would an ordinary family album with snaps of the kids, holidays and days out, only to find it crammed with pornographic images! More revelations followed. It transpired she had lived with her parents on their smallholding, which was also in the village of Bishop's Cleeve. Fred West would do the odd building job around the farm for her father, often inviting the teenager to help him. This she was happy to do since it was much more interesting than homework. One night her parents were out and she was asleep in the house—not knowing that Fred West was beating a path to her bedroom via a ladder. Fortunately for her, but not for West, her father returned home and caught him midway to the window. Papa apparently gave the hopeful Casanova a good hiding and banned him from the homestead. All this came over the phone. An intimate conversation between two people who had never met. Two people who would never meet.

Making notes of our conversation, I arranged to call back after speaking with Central TV. I was convinced the woman's input could make an important contribution to the background item being prepared around the demonic life and times of Herefordshire's most evil son. But we never got to visit the northern resort. The call to her two days later was received with a frostiness that was, in the light of our previous chat, completely unexpected. No warmth this time, just flat refusal. There was no persuading her, no changing her mind. The offer of a donation to her favourite charity, the suggestion of an interview where she could not be identified, were to no avail. She was adamant she would not tell her tale on television.

What had happened in the 48 hours since we first talked by phone, to cause such an about-turn? Were the police in touch with her—did they shut down such an informative avenue? Or was it a husband putting his foot down, embarrassed by the teenage capers of his spouse?

Maybe she decided for herself that she didn't want to be tarnished by the tawdry events being revealed to the world, no matter how long ago. The door to her secrets for a little while so temptingly ajar, was now firmly closed and we had lost the key to open it.

Fatal attraction

As with all things journalistic, the attention span is short-lived. A few days of dramatic mayhem, wrap up the last pieces of the tale, then make a mass exodus to stories new. So it was at Cromwell Street. First the international press departed for Heathrow, taking their foreign accents with them. In their wake followed most of the national papers' staff, stowing away their chequebooks, cobbled expense sheets, cameras and homing to London, ready to cover other news stories, other people's loss and pain. By the end of Spring 1994, all that was left was us locals. We remained watching the fading events because there was nowhere else to go.

We had been there at the very beginning—witnessing the horrific outcome of one police officer's hunch, experiencing all the shocking revelations—and were still there at the end, deserted now by our wider-flung colleagues. Left to see out the final days of a news story so abominable that it almost defied telling but told it had been, and in doing so, had brought the world to our patch.

Fred West, now incarcerated in Birmingham's Winson Green Prison, had a trial and the outcome to look forward to, as did his wife Rosemary, banged-up in Durham goal. 25 Cromwell Street was fenced off, sealed up, a cubic tomb stripped of its dead. 25 Midland Road had been returned to its owners, though the former tenant of the ground floor flat was not to return. (In fact it would be several months before a tenant could be found with nerve enough to make it a home.) Near Much Marcle, the fields, now empty of police, slipped back into natural agricultural use. For me also, the strange season drew to a close, the daily commute to St Michael's Square was over.

By now, two cabinets in Central TV's offices were filled with over 400 video tapes—an epic testament to crimes never to be erased from the minds of the bereaved nor the camera's filmic memory. Cromwell Street was over, but it continued to draw me back. I couldn't break free from the events of the last three months, couldn't stop returning, time after time. It was as a drug, I needed the Cromwell Street 'fix'. Every journey to Gloucester involved a detour to the 'Street of shame'. I would go to the front, check the back, scan the street, chat with locals, trying to make sense of the latest gossip. Any gap in my schedule would find me there. It was impossible to throw off a season's visiting just like that, I was having to slowly wean myself away from the clutches of Cromwell Street. These crazy sorties at first produced nothing but needless diesel pollution and frustration. Yet the visits were not always a waste of time.

I happened upon wreaths, left in the rear garden by thoughtful anonymous souls unconnected to the tragedy but wishing to pay their respects to the dead. On other occasions bouquets appeared as if by magic, secretly left by relatives at the front gates, floral tokens of remembrance to loved ones gone. Then the macabre tale of strangers collecting and bagging up trowelful mementos of earth from the last resting place of the young victims, the deathly soil now in some vase, on some sideboard giving life to a plant in a household of the weird

I watched the graffiti-splashed scrawl on the exterior walls of 25 Cromwell Street being urgently obliterated by council staff before cock-crow, the only other observer the milkman delivering to the sleeping terrace. I witnessed the Germans, the French, the Japanese, the British camera-clicking day trippers arrive by the dozen as though compelled to the Mecca of madness. Smile-focus-snap. Smile-focus-shoot. Saying 'cheese' before a façade of crime. Creating postcards of death for posterity.

My sad addiction to still being there when it seemed to be all over, had, ironically, produced several extra news items during the final tremors of a murderous earthquake that had rocked the city on its very foundations. I eventually laid the ghost of the street and broke away from its lure, or so I thought. But this story was not ready to be cast aside and filed away, it would take on a plot of Shakespearean proportions with its telling. And I would, in future months, find myself again and again and again, returning to Cromwell Street.

Mystery tour

In Hereford, my father, now in his eighties, was seriously ill, diagnosed with cancer, a secret I managed to keep between myself and his doctor. The same illness had taken my mother some seven years previously and he had a dread of the disease and the word. I felt that what spirit he had would be sapped away if he was made aware of his condition, so rightly or wrongly I kept the knowledge from him. His doctor reluctantly agreed with my well-intentioned deceit with the proviso that should my father mention the big C word, he would be told.

I agreed and my father never asked. I think some months before his end he realised his condition and stayed silent to somehow protect me. Father and son, both keeping secrets in the face of death. He still lived in the modest house in Hereford where I had been brought up with him and my mother, who had passed away some eight years earlier. He now shared the family home with his long-time friend, Tom Beddows, who was only a few months younger than my dad. Naturally my father looked forward to my visits, so around work demands I made the journey as often as possible to make sure his last few months were at least comfortable. He always wanted to know what I had been up to and was intrigued by the West murder case. His mind was still alert and he was fascinated with the latest developments in Gloucester murders. During one visit, he expressed great sadness for the victims and turning to me, asked: "What sort of people have you got in Gloucester that can carry out such foul deeds"? I gently pointed out to him that Fred West was a native of our home county, not Gloucestershire.

A fact that he, like the *Sunday Times* reporter before him, had overlooked. He gave no answer, just cast me a wry smile. He was very gentle person and hated any form of cruelty to man or beast but like so many of his era, he was fascinated by crime. He could relate the background to the acid bath murderer Haigh, tell of Ruth Ellis, the last woman to be hanged in England, give you every nuance in the case of Christie carrying out his debauched necrophiliac practices at 10 Rillington Place, detail without hesitation the activities of the poisoner Armstrong, who as a young boy, he saw come to trial at Hereford Assizes. He had also read every Edgar Wallace crime novel several times over. Therefore it was no surprise when he came Cheltenham for a short stay, that he took up my offer of a visit to the district that had daily made headline news over the previous months. So, along with my father and Tom, I joined the rubber-necking Sunday crowds that were still touring the city centre circuit of death. I showed him the various streets and buildings involved in the case.

I pointed out the up-turned garden at Cromwell Street, introduced him to Mr Islam, my Asian friend, made the journey across the park to the vacant apartment in Midland Road. Thus we partook of our very own mystery tour, joining the ranks of gawping tourists that, each weekend, had been drawn as if by magnets, to the street of evil. My father took it all in, storing the images away in his mind, a series of filed facts about a serial killer. Details he would no doubt record, along with his knowledge of Armstrong, Haigh, Ellis and Christie.

Police work in the Cromwell Street district was now over and I spent as much time as possible visiting my father. Despite his rapidly deteriorating physical condition, he was still bright enough of mind always to inquire how the case was proceeding and was eager to learn of the latest developments. With events now in the realm of the legal system, there was little new I could relate, but whenever I entered the cosy front room in which he was now a virtual prisoner, he endeavoured to extract every last detail about the case.

As for so many, the events in the Street of Shame had replaced Eastenders and Coronation Street in the interest ratings. Cromwell Street was the new soap opera and my father, in his final weeks, was as transfixed as the rest of the public. He would greet me with: "Hello son" and almost in the same breath, as if asking after an old friend,: "How's Fred?"

Medicine man

The summer of 1994 was much the same as any other. The occasional fires, road crashes, silly season animal stories, parades, council cuts, demos and holidays. That was until September 12th, when news broke that remains thought to be human had been discovered in a garden by builders carrying out extension work in Cheltenham's Clarence Square. Shocked at their discovery of a skeleton in the grounds of the private nursing home, they alerted police who descended in force on the splendid regency property, situated just 25 yards from where Frederick West had once had a flat in Clarence Street.

The revelation set bells ringing in media offices, bringing the sordid saga of Cromwell Street back to the fore. The scenes of crime team who had attended at Gloucester, arrived in their familiar white van, closely followed by the senior officers of the Cromwell Street inquiry, Detective Superintendent John Bennett and his deputy, Detective Chief Inspector Terry Moore. The builders abandoned work as the police took over the site, taping off the garden and erecting canvas awnings to hide their activities. To us, things looked pretty ominous, especially when a car drew up bearing the Welsh Dragon symbol on the lid of its boot. To us, this confirmed the arrival of Home Office pathologist, Professor Bernard Knight, evidently summoned from Cardiff. With the press presence growing, one could sense all the ingredients needed to put Cromwell Street back to the front pages.

In a hastily cobbled pavement 'presser' (press conference), the media pack were told: "It seems human bones have been revealed at the site. It is too early to establish authenticity. This will be confirmed by Professor Knight's examinations". Our questions trying to link the find to the Cromwell Street inquiry were fielded by silence, followed by a brisk: "That's all Gentlemen".

The next day found us back again, returning to Clarence Square. In some ways not dissimilar to St Michael's in Gloucester, except here the central area was lawn, not car park, and the surrounding houses occupied by wealthy private residents, as opposed to an itinerant flow of bedsit dwellers. The two squares started out pretty much the same, providing elegant homes for those with enough money to buy them. But fate took the areas down two different paths and, in this instance, fate was kinder to Clarence Square.

The skeleton unearthed in the nursing home garden was human, but there all similarity to events in Gloucester ended, the result of a strand of copper wire. Professor Knight concluded that the discovery was a discarded anatomical model that had probably once belonged to a doctor or medical student. The discovery of tiny holes in the bones, coupled with various pieces of wire, confirmed Knight's suspicions that the now-discarded human frame was not the result of a foul deed. The builders' macabre find was as simple as that. Ironically, the rather worn out skeleton had probably been buried to avoid the very alarm it was now causing. The fuss over, the reserved residents of Cheltenham Spa's Clarence Square could step back from their window-watching to sip a sherry, prepare for dinner and express a communal sigh of relief.

West end

They were two different men. One a monster, the other majestic. They both suffered a traumatic death. One by his own hand, leaving mysteries unsolved and a police force shocked. The other, killed for reasons unknown, leaving a world stunned. Two very different men with a thirty year gap in their departure, brought together only by their unforgettable exit from earth. Folk of my age group will always tell you what they were doing or where they were in November 1963, when President Kennedy was assassinated.

It's etched in the mind, a televisual image of such moment it cannot fade. I was working with a reporter from the *Sunday Mirror* in one of the less salubrious areas of Cheltenham, covering an alleged case of police brutality against some mother's son. Competing with the strident noise of a gurgling television, the reporter was desperately trying to sort fact from fiction from a mother whose yobbo lad 'could do no wrong', but did. As the woman was in full flow on the topic of the 'bastard police', a news flash appeared on the television screen. My companion, looking up, yelled at the mother to be quiet as we stared at the image of a blood-stained Jackie Kennedy clutching her dying husband's head to her chest. Even if the Cheltenham story had stood up, which it didn't, it would never make next-day's pages now, thanks to the terrible happenings in Texas. People still tell of that unforgettable day in America's history, how they were cooking dinner, driving home, making love, having a row, reading a book, when the clocks paused in America.

It was New Year's Day 1995, that no man's land time when nothing happens. Christmas over, the remains of the turkey a shambles in the fridge, presents discarded. The anticlimax to festivities beginning to turn stale. Unless of course you were Scottish. In fact it was no-news time with thin bulletins to match.

I was on standby for Central TV as reports came in of an unfortunate New Year's Eve calamity in a Cirencester pub. A group of female revellers had transformed themselves with liberal dabs of cotton wool and glue into a fancy-dress flock of sheep. The young girls done up as mutton, visited their local inn and were naturally, the centre of attention. The fun was short-lived. One of the boisterous onlookers making jokes about roast lamb, flicked his cigarette lighter, causing the spirit-glued costumes to ignite and engulf the merrymakers. Shocked customers struggled to put out the flames but sadly it was from hospital beds that some of the girls sheepishly saw in the New Year. While roaming the streets of Cirencester for information about the unlucky accident, I answered my mobile to hear the shocking news of Fred West's suicide.

He had hanged himself by a home-made rope of plaited sheeting, secretly constructed within the privacy of his Winson Green cell. The jail's notorious guest had finally decided to leave this world. Everyone was caught off guard by Fred's unbelievable two-fingered gesture to society. Family, police, prison and press. It was so out of character, so out of the blue. One minute bragging, grinning, mocking authority, defying logic, confusing the system, offering solutions.

The next minute gone. Leaving a vacuum so massive in the police inquiries, it could never be filled. The hoped-for fountain of information had dried up. Drained of life on the end of a few knotted prison sheets.

New Year's Day and every news desk in the country was running on skeleton staff and most of those, suffering an excess of festive spirit. For all of us, getting our act together was a major effort. Still reeling from the shock news, Central's reporter, Gareth Furby and I abandoned the Cirencester sheep story and raced towards Gloucester, mobile phones red-hot as we pulled the facts into shape.

ITN national news wanted as much as we could get for the evening programme and we had little to go on. There was only one place to make for and, after a seven-month gap, we returned to Cromwell Street. We arrived in darkness as the street was beginning to fill with media and inquisitive locals. We fought against the clock, desperately trying to grab interviews and opinions from bewildered residents, many of whom weren't aware that Fred was dead. Our work was further frustrated as most of the folk we had come to know over the preceding months had either disappeared in moonlight flits or moved on to improve their lot. We were left chatting up strangers who knew little or nothing of Fred West.

Known in the trade as vox pops, the on-street sound bite opinions from passing strangers about current events are a nightmare to obtain and dreaded by TV crews. Out of six such interviews, only about one or two are normally usable. That is if you are lucky enough to get six! Most folk, shy of camera and mike when confronted, make such excuses as: 'in a hurry', 'don't know', 'have no idea', 'must get back to work'.

Anything rather than possibly make a fool of themselves or give a valued opinion. Of those who will talk, much is libellous and has to be scrapped, others deviate wildly from the question, their strangulated answers adding up to further unusable nonsense. It is not easy suddenly finding a microphone thrust into your face demanding an instant interpretation, one can understand their embarrassment, but its uncanny how all the world's barrack-room lawyers disappear when you need them.

Cromwell Street was no different in this regard and vital minutes were lost seeking out responses to Fred West's fate. With the congregation exiting from the evening service in the next-door church to the Wests' former home, we prayed for a statement from the religions elders. After much deliberation they answered our request with 'no comment'. Even God's earthbound spokesmen were reluctant to offer words of forgiveness or any words at all, regarding a one-time neighbour. The night was eventually saved with a garbled interview from a passing gentleman of no fixed abode, coupled with another resident's opinion, 'He's done us all a favour'.

The film package was finally wrapped with a brief and to-the-point police statement underlining the known facts of Fred West's death and the whole was pumped electronically down the line to a panicking ITN newsroom. Only then could we, still reeling from the news, take stock of the dramatic outcome on the year's first day of 1995.

Chief Superintendent John Bennett and his Cromwell Street inquiry team were stunned to the point of pure shock. How could the most central figure to the whole investigation, have been allowed such latitude—tearing up sheets to be woven into rope, reinforced with stitched cotton—under the eyes of his prison guards. It defied credibility. Everyone bound to the Cromwell Street nightmare was staggered by the outcome of events in a prison of England's third most important city. Anne Marie, Fred's daughter, who was regularly visiting her father in his Birmingham gaol, knew nothing of the drama that was unfolding on New Year's day. Wrapped up in the domesticity of her young family she listened neither to radio or television.

While the media, armed with the knowledge of her father's death, was beating a path to Cromwell Street, she was indoors playing with her children and preparing meals with her boyfriend Phil, unaware of the growing turmoil in the street where she had once lived. It took a relative on her step-mother's side, in a late evening phone call, to cruelly break the news. This tormented young woman, who in later months would prove to be so majestic in the face of adversity, was mortified. In spite of his terrible history and vicious treatment of her, she had stood by him throughout, regardless of his monstrous acts — he was still her father. To ease the pain and the shock of being one of the last to know his fate, she turned to drink and tablets, the dreadful combination of which involved a panic race to Gloucester Hospital and the ignominy of the stomach pump. Tim Hurst, Central Television's chief Gloucestershire reporter, who had been on the Cromwell Street story since spades turned over the first sods in the back garden, was taking a well-earned Christmas break from the rigours of news.

He'd rented a cottage in Cornwall, no radio, no television, no papers. A festive news blackout, cutting himself and his wife off from the world of woe, relying on good food, good books and fine claret to see them through the season of goodwill. It was at a motorway service station, on his way home two days later, that he learned of the death of Frederick West. He bought every paper he could lay hands on, soaked up the headlines and column inches. An hour later he was still parked on the garage forecourt, stunned rigid. The following day, various members of Central's reporting staff, though still technically on holiday, found themselves wandering back to the Gloucester office. They arrived as if pre-tuned, unable to keep away from the unfolding drama, needing to be involved, compelled back to Gloucester.

Fred West left this world with a million secrets, or none. He was a serial killer *par excellence*, or a much-maligned man protecting others. He left his captors to decide.

His dangling death closed unknown doors to unsolved mysteries.

Body count

At the height of the Cromwell Street inquiry, detectives had come to accept that every missing woman logged on the nationwide files was a potential victim of Fred West. This dreadful prospect was underlined by Fred's nomadic existence. He had worked in Scotland as well as the North of England, had been employed in the Midlands and the West Country. His known victims had been plucked from a variety of diverse locations—Swiss student, Therese Siegenthaler for example, was picked up while hitch-hiking to Devon from her London base.

So it was not an illogical possibility: the police already knew that Fred was a serial killer but how prolific his evil was could not be measured. The facts tell of twelve deaths including his first wife Catherine, buried in a Gloucestershire field and their baby daughter, Charmaine, found under concrete at Gloucester's Midland Road. Many serving police officers, and others now retired, are convinced that despite lack of proof and West's denials, he was also responsible for the disappearance of Mary Bastholm in 1968.

They believe she was one of his early victims, like Ann McFall, whose murder he was charged with but for some perverse and inexplicable reason—as with Mary— to which he would never admit when questioned. During the murder investigations someone high in police circles uttered startling words during an informal chat on the case: "We know more or less how many victims he has coughed to, we know the end came when he was arrested, but when did he start? There's a great gap after 1978 when Shirley Anne Robinson went missing, right up to 1987 when Heather was last seen, then another period up to his arrest in 1994. So who else did he kill? Serial killers don't stop—they go on and on". Chilling thoughts indeed from a man in the know. Should there be other victims from Cromwell Street, and there is a strong possibility of it, there is only one person who now may hold the key: Rose West.

Perhaps one day she can be persuaded to shed light on the whole grim chapter but the fact that she has remained silent throughout, does not encourage any such optimism. To establish that Fred West was the most prolific serial killer in British history is now virtually impossible, though many officers in the Gloucestershire force are of the mind he could well have been the holder of this diabolical record.

Death knell

The furore over the death of Fred West ran on for the rest of the week and well into the next. Winson Green prison, understandably in the circumstances, said little and a frustrated Gloucestershire police force remained tight-lipped for fear of venting real feelings. The press turned to the family for comments on his exit from this life and awaited the next act, his funeral. West's daughter, Anne Marie, was planning to organise the arrangements, saying from the outset that, as a mark of respect, she wished to see all the murder victims laid to rest before her father was buried. Sadly her wish would not be fulfilled.

The funeral of Fred West was an impossible, and some might say thankless, task. It was said that some undertakers had refused to handle the ceremony, not because of what he had been accused of, but because of his infamy.

They foresaw that press and pandemonium could well be the order of the day should news of the funeral get out. Anne Marie West was expecting to handle the occasion. She had, after all, been the relative who had formally identified her late father in the Birmingham mortuary. She thought she had things under control: she wanted dignity for the victims followed by a resemblance of dignity for her dad. But her wishes were to be dashed. As Fred's body lay in the mortuary, plans were already afoot to spirit the corpse away to a secret place. Other members of the family arranged to have the body released into their custody and in the twinkling of an eye, he was gone. This dramatic deed further split the already divided West clan and threw the media into a crematorial panic. Convinced that Fred West's funeral was only days if not hours away, they worked on the premise that whoever was in charge of the ceremony, along with *The Sun* newspaper who held exclusive rights to the occasion, would never risk holding it in Gloucestershire. There was no way they could guarantee exclusivity that close to home. Therefore the uninformed papers and TV stations staked out possible options within a 40-mile radius of Birmingham, plus a few extra for good measure. Many cameramen were dispatched around the West Country to face lonely churchyard vigils. I got Gloucester Crematorium. For two days I watched cortège after cortège arrive at the imposing façade. A depressing stream of black vehicles disgorging weeping mourners, unloading coffin after coffin, but not Fred West.

It was on the afternoon of Wednesday 29th March we heard the news, Lanley Crematorium near Coventry, was host to the unwelcome guest. The service was led by Reverend Robert Simpson, the vicar at Newent, a small town some ten miles from Gloucester. He had been approached by an undertaker, asking that he take the service while also keeping the date and venue secret. This he promised to do.

"I understood that Fred West had named his son Stephen executor, hence he was in charge of the funeral arrangements", said Reverend Simpson. "As a vicar, I felt it was a job that had to be done and undertook the task without question. When I arrived at the crematorium I met up with a small group of family members awaiting my arrival. I must say I was quite surprised to find a few camera-carrying members of the media there." He continued: "It's now some twenty years since this all took place. The memory has faded a little but the service as I remember, was a quiet unassuming occasion carried out in the way funerals are. With the exception of a few surprising flashguns going off, it was otherwise a normal funeral service, only the name Fred West made it an unusual occasion." The Reverend Simpson is now retired and still living in Gloucestershire.

Silence in court

For a whole week during the February of 1995, Fred West and the tragedy of his victims came back to haunt Gloucestershire during his wife's pre-trial hearing held at Dursley magistrates' court.

Rose West was charged with ten murders. The object of this legal exercise was to establish whether she had a case to answer at a full trial. There was little doubt in most people's minds but the law had to take its course. The neat town on the south-west edge of the Cotswold escarpment was prepared for a press invasion.

The courtrooms adjacent to the police station had been cordoned off by the council with protective fencing and police were in charge of a security system to check all court arrivals. The media reporters had to apply for special passes to attend the main body of the court, while the less favoured made do with a tannoyed annexe from which to cover proceedings. The local school provided car-parking in their sports field and refreshments in the pavilion, the income adding to school funds. The sports ground bloomed with antennas bouncing story signals to stations worldwide. England was the only country in the world not allowed to publish the courtroom revelations for fear of prejudicing the eventual trial.

Brits would have to await the Winchester hearing in November before the gruesome facts rendered them speechless. Rose West, on each of her visits to court, made an invisible but nevertheless gladiatorial entrance into the town, hidden from view in a blacked-out prison vehicle, flanked by police motorcycle outriders.

Daily we filmed her arrival and departure —to be honest, just the vehicles coming and going for we saw nothing of her inside the speeding van as she arrived from, and returned to, Pucklechurch Remand Centre. The British journalists, crammed cheek-by-jowl in the packed courthouse, took notes and listened to lurid facts they could not tell or write of. Witnesses to terror, gagged by the vagaries of British law into silence while their foreign colleagues pumped news and pictures worldwide, unhindered by such restrictions.

For the media outside, the only happening of any moment occurred when youths threw eggs at the vehicle transporting Rose West. Twelve months into the inquiry was this to before the first outbreak of genuine Gloucestershire anger? Might this be the real sign of public feelings coming at last to the surface? No way. Rumours said the yobs were egged on by newspaper men. Most of the missiles missed the van and splattered into the onlookers. Several reporters ended up with egg on their faces.

Death watch

By the very nature of the work, death features largely in a journalist's life. Other people's passing. Death by accident, death by misadventure, death by natural causes, death by murder. After the street-watching, after the door-knocking, after the sympathetic discussion in the front parlour, there are the funerals. Local papers attend each one, methodically listing every mourner, a tally of mourners that will find prominence in the next editions. Should the deceased, in life, have had fame thrust upon them, they will be immortalised in death, as the national press scramble among the wreaths and bouquets, noting who has written what, on the floral tributes.

There will always be funerals. I attended Sir Winston Churchill's service at Bladon church, standing alongside Jackie Kennedy in the rain-drenched mountains of North Wales, as Lord Harlech took his last journey. Watched grief-stricken Rolling Stones fans hanging over the open grave of Brian Jones as they said their last goodbyes. Fell in step with the Gloucester Regiment as they marched through the Cotswold town of Winchcombe when they buried one of their own, cut down by Belfast bullets. Watched the pathetic cloth-wrapped bundle of a still-born baby lowered coffinless into the ochre-red earth in Sierra Leone. Glimpsed a distant flag-draped coffin as the Duke of Windsor was quietly returned to English soil. Life's great leveller is death. Peer or peasant the end result is the same. Regardless of their status on earth they each take the same journey, leaving the same pain for loved ones left.

Anne Marie West's bereavement was exceptionally long-delayed. She had to wait some twenty-four years before she could lay to rest her mother, Catherine and her sister Charmaine. She finally found peace for her shattered family in Kettering Cemetery during April 1995. Through sheer journalistic prowess, Central TV's Ken Goodwin, got to know Anne Marie in the early days of the Cromwell Street story. He became a confidante, a friend to the tormented young mother struggling to come to terms with the wretchedness that life was throwing at her through her father's terrible deeds. Anne Marie was later to be contracted exclusively to the *Daily Star*, but she never forgot the sympathetic support Ken Goodwin had shown. She insisted, where possible without compromising her agreement with the paper, that he would be involved in the outcome as it developed.

So that's how we came to be in Kettering on a bright spring morning, in company with Detective Superintendent John Bennett and members of his team, also paying their last respects. Anne Marie organised the occasion with all the care and thought she could muster, choosing Kettering as a convenient location between her own home and her late mother's Scottish relatives, far enough from Gloucester to avoid a mass media presence. Determined, after the scramble of her father's departure, that her mother and sister would be laid to rest with dignity.

The cortège consisted of two sets of remains but only one coffin. Anne Marie's wishes were that mother and daughter, cruelly separated in life, would be reunited in death. With the grace of a duchess, in a tailored black suit with subdued black hat and veil, she mingled with her new-found distant relatives. The occasional gesture of a white handkerchief wiping her eyes, otherwise totally in control, proffering a kiss here, a comforting hand there, making awkward funereal small talk with sympathetic skill. This was not the Anne Marie who nearly drank and overdosed herself into oblivion some months ago, this was a woman with a duty she had steeled herself to fulfil and she did so admirably, with quiet decorum. After a quarter of a century she was at last able to lay the ghost of her lost sister alongside the memories of her lost mother.

Desecration

Within a couple of weeks of the Kettering funerals we were back in the Herefordshire village of Much Marcle, the former childhood home of Fred West, following another twist in this dark tale. Furtive glances and twitching curtains at various windows, alerted us to the fact that our presence was not going unnoticed by the inhabitants of this pretty rural backwater. That we were not welcome was obvious. Our casual smiles were rebuffed. As far as the locals were concerned, questions were out of the question. No one was prepared to talk with us regarding anything Fred West. It was if he had never existed. To a person they wished him a million miles away. The reason for our unwanted return was the macabre activities on the previous night, when unseen by any of the all-seeing residents, some members of the community had descended on the lovely English churchyard and irreligiously uprooted the headstones of Daisy and Walter West. As teeth pulled by a dentist, the marble plaques were wrenched from the gums of the grave, despoiling the final resting place of Fred's parents.

A pointless act of vandalism had thrust the villagers back into the headlines, rekindling events they were desperate to put to the back of their minds. The nocturnal gravestone vandals were never discovered, nor the tombstones, though it was strongly hinted around those parts that they lay at the bottom of a nearby pond. Rough rural justice dealt out of frustration? More probably a caper fuelled by the excellent strong cider brewed within the district of Much Marcle. The sins of a son visited upon a father and mother.

No problem

How often are those words mouthed, 'no problem'? A third-world expression used in excess across Africa and the Middle East to ease every situation. An international expression that solves everything. 'want taxi—no problem', 'want fair price—no problem', 'want good woman—no problem'. The problem is, there are always problems, even in England.

My friend and camera colleague, Les Leach told me over a coffee break, that he had been approached, while filming in Gloucester, by a scallywag offering to get him inside 25 Cromwell Street,. "Just bring a ladder and £250 quid in cash, no problem".

Having seen how the Wests' property had been sealed up, we both agreed he was a rogue and not to be trusted. Yet it puzzled me how he could be so cocksure, so confident. We had witnessed the windows and doors being bricked up, the steel sheet welded across the apertures, a walled-up catacomb with no way in or out. I wandered round the now-abandoned house. Everything seemed intact, the odd fence was broken down, clues that there had been intruders, but otherwise solid to the outside world, no visible sign of a breach in the abode-turned-fortress. Word on the street was that certain newspapers had already crossed the threshold into the Wests' former home, courtesy of the untrained surveyor, but the locals knew not how. It is said for every new burglar alarm there are twenty crooks working out ways to beat the system, for every new locking device, an army of thieves dedicated to breaking the code.

Could this be so at Cromwell Street? The police had gone to tremendous lengths to secure the property. The devious had gone to outstanding lengths to get in—and had done so. The criminal mind had applied lateral thinking to the challenge. No way in the front, top, back or bottom, but how about sideways? Next door to number twenty-five was a derelict semi-sister of the Wests' house, left neglected by its owners, rear windows ajar, the frames hanging from broken hinges. Everything pointed to this being the way of entry into the murderous maze. Climb into number twenty-seven, knock a hole through the wall to twenty-five … hey presto!

But if you could walk from lounge to lounge or bedroom to bedroom via a gaping hole, why the ladder? Simple. Take the stairs to the top floor, rest the ladder into the roof space and cross the roofing joists. Reverse the procedure to join the sad spirits in the basement below. That was how the criminal fraternity outwitted the police. With a vertical ladder and lateral interpretation.

Having followed their thinking, worked out their route, the door to the House of Horrors was open to me—and without having to find the £250. To say I was not tempted would be to lie. I wanted to go in, to experience for myself the interior of hell denied to us all. My God was I tempted. For days I mulled it over, weighing up the possible outcome. There was no doubt in my mind that I would achieve photographic success by making the eerie pilgrimage. As the man said, 'no problem' It was neither fear of the dark unknown nor threat of arrest that held me back, in themselves both persuasive reasons. What brought me to my senses was that, if caught, it would ruin thirty years of goodwill with Gloucestershire police, All would be rendered worthless by one reckless midnight caper. The value of being the local man would be destroyed by a single foolish action. Trespass I could live with, even arrest would be an experience but being declared *persona non grata* on my own territorial doorstep would be unforgivable. Reluctantly, so very reluctantly, I walked away from the beckoning broken window that led into the House of Horrors.

I left it for others to experience the adrenalin rush as they traversed the creaking roof space. Months later, in October 1995, when police were preparing the house for the famous Winchester jury visit, the tell-tale sign of discarded film canisters littering the cellar floor spoke of their visitations.

Mary Bastholm as bridesmaid at her brother Peter's wedding. Photograph issued by police when she disappeared in 1968

Constable John Bennett, a member of Gloucestershire police sub-aqua team, preparing to dive Gloucester canal in 1968 during the search for Mary Bastholm. On the left, Detective Superintendent Bill Marchant of Scotland Yard, in charge of the Bastholm enquiry

Mary's brother, Peter Bastholm, who was flown home to the UK from his ship when Mary went missing

A *Gloucester Citizen* 'read all about it' billboard outside a corner shop near Cromwell Street

A police-issued photograph of Lucy Partington, who vanished from a
Cheltenham bus stop in December 1973

**Overalled Police Divisional Support Group team pictured here during a break
at the Cromwell Street search**

Detective Chief Inspector Terry Moore and (right) Detective Superintendent John Bennett in the rear garden of Cromwell Street on the day the property was finally sealed up

The final days of the Wests' former home—demolished and removed from the
street for ever, then buried metres below a landfill site on the edge of
Gloucester city

Blood brother

To meet Douglas West one could see the likeness. He carried the same thickset build and spoke with the same rural accent. He lived and worked where he was born, in the village of Much Marcle, along with his wife and four children. Like many men in the small community, he worked the land. Besides the pub, the village store, the cider factory and garage, there was little choice. A man of the soil, farming stock, steeped in the lore of country ways. But having compared the likeness between Fred and Doug West, there the similarities ended. Doug had none of Fred's arrogance, no boastful tone in conversation. A gentle-natured man, he could have been happy with his lot in life but for one overwhelming factor: the sins of his brother.

Along with his family he had faced the hordes of journalists knocking at his cottage door seeking insights into the twilight world of Fred. He had coped with lengthy police inquiries, come to terms with the dreadful tally of victims and the final shock of his brother's ignominious end. Yet as you listened to his voice with, its that warm Herefordshire tones, weighing up answers to endless questions you could detect a trace of disappointment when he talked of the village. It seemed that some folk who had known him all his life, who once were happy to swap rural small talk, now stayed on the other side of the highway to avoid conversation. Understandably, many were no doubt embarrassed into silence, unable to find the right words. Others perhaps took the view that the West family were all 'tarred with the same brush' and closed their minds to reason. For Douglas, the animosity was hurtful, something he could not comprehend. For he had done nothing wrong. He aided the police in every way possible, expressed great compassion regarding the dead and was resigned to the terrible burden of being Fred's brother.

Bewilderment was etched on his face as he detailed the attitude of his peers and one could not but feel sorry for his predicament. He was the Doug West they had always known, he worked, paid his bills, tended his family. He was no different. Still the same Doug West they had chatted to and swilled pints with. There might have been some sanctuary from the whispering and pointing fingers had he lived in a crowded city, but he was trapped in a tight-knit community of country dwellers, surrounded by wagging tongues and gossip. Through no fault of his own, Doug West found folk ignoring him for being the brother of Fred. He inherited a loathsome Cain and Abel legacy which only time might ease

Femme fatale

It was considered that Catherine Costello (known as Rena), Fred West's first wife, was dead before he came to know Rosemary Letts. Believed that Rosemary did not arrive on the scene until sometime after the disappearance of Catherine from the caravan dwelling she shared with Fred and her two daughters, Anne Marie and Charmaine at Bishop's Cleeve village near Cheltenham.

Time has clouded details, for these events took place in October 1969. The comings and goings of Fred and Catherine at the time were mobile to say the least. Towards the end of that October, well over forty years ago, Catherine leaves West and the children, not for the first time, to travel back to her Scottish home. The reason for this hurried departure we will never know. A week later, social services call at the caravan and find a young girl looking after Charmaine and Anne Marie. Unhappy with the situation, the authorities take the two youngsters into care. In the middle of November, Catherine arrives back in Bishop's Cleeve and the family is reunited. Only three days pass before Catherine again leaves the caravan, signalling another spell in care for the confused children caught up in this domestic disarray. More intriguing is the identity of the young female babyminder noted by social services during their visit? Could she have been the future Rose West?

It's quite feasible because eight days after Catherine left for the last time, Rose Letts reached her sixteenth birthday and a short while later moved into the caravan vacated by Fred's first wife. Is it possible that Catherine's frequent flights from the family home were brought on by jealousy? Fred's oversexed attentions to the attractive teenager sparking exodus upon exodus by the older woman? Was Rose Letts, at the age of sweet sixteen, an innocent bystander caught up in events beyond her control, manipulated by an older man? Or is it likely she was the puppeteer, pulling the strings, bending Fred to her will with impassioned sexual favours? For sure, history is littered with such powerful women.

Within twelve months, Fred, Charmaine, and Anne Marie, along with his now-pregnant partner, Rose Letts, vacate the mobile home in favour of a flat at 25 Midland Road, Gloucester. It was there that the result of their caravan coupling—the baby to be named Heather—was born. From the front door of their Midland Road flat, it was possible to see Cromwell Street just across the park, where years later their baby named Heather would die.

So Rose joins Fred and just over a year later Fred and Rose become enjoined. They married at Gloucester Register Office but there is no recorded mention of a divorce between Fred West and his wife Catherine. In the eyes of the law he was a bigamist, yet he couldn't be, for Catherine was dead. No not a bigamist, a murderer. Now the groom and bride move to a new home, 25 Cromwell Street, just a short walk from their flat in Midland Road, where his daughter, Charmaine, was now entombed under the kitchen floor. Together, Fred and Rose, within the four walls and three floors of Cromwell Street would fulfil their perverted sexual fantasies, perpetrate ungodly acts on God knows how many. How do two such people come together, what accident of destiny decrees the meeting of minds and bodies so vile, so sexually deviant that it defies logic?. If only we knew. That sex was the motivator is undeniable. An insatiable man meets his equal in woman, the die is cast. They enjoy first each other, then others. And so the lust is unleashed, the cravings uncontrolled.

New tricks are required to sate the sexual hunger, but the longing remains unsated. Sadism augments the sex in the downward spiral for fresh kicks. Inflict the pain, experience the pleasure. But one day a participant is unwilling, threatens the very existence of the game by resisting, finding no enjoyment in the sordid sport. Now Fred and Rose become as one, diabolically fused when confronted with the dilemma: they invest in the insurance policy of death. But who voices the idea? Who makes the suggestion? The first move? How do you ask your partner in life to even consider such deeds of death, without fear they will run headlong to the law? How do you voice the vile idea with the confidence it will stay secret? One of them did. Amazingly they found feelings mutual. No furtive calls to the police, no hurried night-time escape, no revulsion. Acceptance. Of all the humans roaming the earth, they found each other, joining to create a partnership designed in hell, two mortals destined by the devil to be paired.

A marriage in murder now inextricably entwined. The bond had been made. There would be no return from the chosen path, like Hindley and Brady before them, they had entered the abyss.

Snapshots

The first day of Rose Pauline West's trial at Winchester was on 3rd October 1995 where she pleaded not guilty to any of the ten charges of murder. For the prosecution it was the culmination of twenty months' work. Nearly two years had passed since the fateful day in February 1994 when Detective Constables, Darren Law and Hazel Savage had knocked on the door of 25 Cromwell Street. Little did they know then the inquiry into the whereabouts of one person would end in a total of twelve. All female, all missing, all murdered. The climax to the whole mind-blowing series of events was about to take place, and the beautiful city of Winchester braced itself for the explosion. Despite several IRA hearings, this was the biggest legal battle since the treason trial of Sir Walter Raleigh in 1603. The impressive large courtyard swarmed on day one with journalists, cameramen and photographers, their paraphernalia draped from railings and piled on walkways. Power cables snaked across pavements, tripods secured coveted viewpoints, news readers talked to themselves, rehearsing opening lines, statements that would flash across Great Britain and the world through the magic of satellite. The good people of Winchester added to the mayhem, a fascinated crowd watching the media circus prepare for its daily performance— dramatic acts that would last until the middle of November. Despite its vast size it was impossible for the Crown Court to provide every press seat application so overspill facilities were arranged in adjacent rooms for the less fortunate scribes. They had to make do with tannoy sound systems relaying the courtroom proceedings, blind to the body language of witness and accused. We outside, were deaf and blind to the wheel of justice slowly turning in the house of law.

Unlike our privileged colleagues, there was no chance of watching criminal history in the making. We were to record the daily comings and goings from outside the precincts of the court, obtaining footage to fill the sandwiches of news fed to a mesmerised nation. We accepted the chore—filming the prison gates as Rose West left each morning secure inside a cage, the cage inside the van. Filming the van's arrival at the Court. Filming the judge, outflanked by a police motorcycle escort, as he alighted from his car. Filming the defence barristers. Filming the prosecution barristers. Filming the crowds. Filming ourselves. At close of day, the exercise was repeated .. the exodus recorded, the same as in the morning but in reverse. Then and only then did we get respite—find a meal, take a drink, chew the fat, go to bed. Slip into sleep knowing that tomorrow will be a mirror image of today. If my tone suggests some reluctance on my part, it's not meant. I wanted to be at Winchester and was fortunate that Central TV afforded me the opportunity to see the story through to its end. But if Cromwell Street was dramatic for cameraman, Winchester for a cameraman was an anticlimax. The trial was the reporters' domain, requiring the medium of voice and language to paint pictures of courtroom scenes and emotions. Words were the strength of the coverage, the journalist told his transfixed audience what they needed to know, the camera was just a necessary appendix.

Photographically, court cases are not the easiest of assignments. Parking is always difficult yet all eventualities have to be covered. Camera, tripod, battery lights, microphone, spare tapes, spare batteries, warm clothes, waterproof camera cover, mobile phone. All have to be traipsed from car to courthouse and watched like a hawk. Having settled on your pitch, you wait. There are vast tracts of time when nothing happens and the cafés down the road seem so inviting. But to leave is madness, for court cases are extremely unpredictable. A sudden change of plea or a dramatic courtroom delivery can send the reporters scurrying to their mobile phones and camera positions.

So you stand your ground through a British climate that can sometimes combine four seasons in one day. After the initial excitement of meeting with old colleagues and swapping anecdotes, coupled with occasional friendly banter with passing pretty girls, there is nothing but the waiting. Unlike America and many European countries, cameras are forbidden in British courts. To further frustrate the situation every court has its own precincts—zones within which no photographer is allowed to stand. The attitude to these external strictures has relaxed over the years and photographers at some courts are more readily accepted within these areas, but the modernisation of many court buildings has created other problems. Most of the major Crown Courts have installed vast automatic doors leading to a sealed-off yard, affording protection for both witness and accused from the camera's eye. The vehicles ferrying the sought-after passengers now generally have darkened windows, hiding their occupants from view .

As a consequence, a daily cat-and-mouse game develops twixt press and the prison vans as they arrive and depart at court. Snappers raise motor-driven Nikons to the van's windows in a futile attempt to capture an image. On the first day at Winchester, as Rose West was being driven back to prison, several photographers chased the van up the road, desperate 'get one in the bag'. It was to no avail. One over-zealous snapper got too close to the accelerating vehicle. Its huge wing mirror caught his shoulder, bowling him across the Winchester highway to the delight of the onlooking crowd. He picked himself up none the worse for his caper, only to find himself featuring on the evening news courtesy of the BBC.

Amazingly, these useless gestures are sometimes successful. Three days into the trial, the 9am ritual again swung into action with a media crowd outside the prison to record the departure of the Rose West courtroom cavalcade. Just as the van and its police escort came through the prison gates, an ambulance with blue lights flashing, emerged from the hospital opposite. The van driver had no choice but to halt, straddled across the highway.

Seizing a golden opportunity, the press pounced. All the waiting, all the pointless chasing paid off as a battery of flashguns 'monstered' the vehicle, urgently seeking out its devilish cargo. Despite this blip in the well-oiled police routine, there was no guarantee of success for the press corps attack. The cameras fired off blind, desperately thrust at the tinted windows, camera'-s loaded with film and a little optimism. Sensing a change in their luck, those at the scene descended on the local 'one hour' photo shop and prayed. Whoever is the patron saint of snappers answered their prayers. By some miracle, the flashguns penetrated the thick smoke-toned glass, lasered across the interior of the van and illuminated the inner cage to freeze the stunned image of Rose West. The startled, unflattering 'portrait' made the front page of most of the next day's tabloids.

After initial coverage of the opening few days of the media-dubbed 'trial of the century', I was to return to Gloucestershire, leaving colleagues to face the remaining weeks of rain, wind, and occasional autumnal sunshine, interspersed with long bouts of boredom. I was not to return until the judge's summing up

Flight times

The bird's-eye angle frequently used by picture editors to provide a different slant on stories featured heavily in the Cromwell Street coverage. In the early weeks, fixed-wing aircraft buzzed the area daily in attempts to capture the layout of the number 25 and the surrounding district. Height flying restrictions limited the success of these initial ventures, the long garden edged by tall fir trees and church walls, made it difficult to obtain good detail from a thousand feet, so eventually the media turned to the more versatile helicopter. Although expensive, cost was the least of their worries and the outlay was justified by the superior images obtained from the hovering craft.

The choppers came back with a vengeance when police work was completed at Cromwell Street and moved the few hundred yards to start digging and searching at Midland Road. There was no peace from the buzzing aircraft at Much Marcle either. As the excavation grew larger, so the planes increased in number. When Rose West was taken on her first journey from Winchester Prison to the austere dock in the Crown Court, her progress were followed from the air. ITN News hovered above the scene, the helicopter fitted with the latest system of hydraulic camera suspension to iron out vibration and air pockets. That night's viewers watched the smooth film passage of Mrs West's phalanx move through the winding streets of Winchester right up to the steel portals of justice. These flying escapades reached their zenith on October 19th 1995, this the day chosen for the visit of judge and jury to what had now become Britain's most tarnished address, 25 Cromwell Street.

As Mr Justice Mantell climbed into his chauffeur-driven limousine and the jury boarded an air-conditioned luxury coach its curtained windows hiding its occupants from the world, they were not know they had company. Three hundred feet above them, ITN's state-of-the-art eye-in-the-sky videoed every manoeuvre of the 73-mile trip, making legal history on its journey to the former home of

Fred and Rose West. Gloucestershire police force had gone to tremendous efforts to provide the Winchester Court with every detail of the property that they might require in their deliberations. The force exhibition officer, PC Eric Williams, spent six months constructing a 20:1 scale model of the house in plywood and balsa. This doll's house of death, designed in a way that it could be dismantled to allow views of every aspect, also displayed colour-coded stages of the extension work completed over the years by its obsessive DIY owner. In addition to these model-making skills, scores of photographs plus two- and three-dimensional plans of all three murder sites were on hand for perusal.

The judge indicated that he did not feel the jury needed to visit Gloucester, but the eleven good men and women (one of the jurors was relieved of his service during the trial) had other ideas. Maybe they desired a break from the almost unbearable daily details they faced .. or felt it was imperative to experience the seat of the crimes for themselves. Who knows? But make the journey they did, creating further burdens for the overstretched local force.

Men who had put Cromwell Street behind them for ever found themselves back on the scene, as the garden was laid to gravel and a specially-constructed steel gate was installed at the back lane to seal off the rear entrance. A huge marquee was erected covering the whole area. To any passing stranger, it would appear that an upmarket function was being planned—it was only the district that beggared such belief. Where parts of the property had been demolished in the search for bodies, white tapes and paint marked the outline of the original structures. The bricked-up front doorway was re-opened and the interior lighting made to work.

With police guards back and front, Cromwell Street, spick and span, was ready to receive its judicial visitors. And so it was on that same day that the street summoned us again—it seemed we would never leave the terrace, doomed forever to wander the depressing district. The pavements of St Michael's Square, the route chosen to bring the judge and jury into the rear of the property, were now lined with metal barricades, manned by an army of police who had cleared the highway of traffic for the motorcade. We did not need to be tipped off about the coach party's arrival—ITN's helicopter did that, swinging over the Gloucester city skyline with its rotor blades pitched to hold it on the course of its prey. Seconds later the phantom charabanc with its heavily curtained windows swept into the square and disappeared inside the envelope of canvas, readied for its presence.

As we attempted to record these latest dramas, Mr Justice Mantell was discreetly guided into the silent building via the adjacent Gloucestershire Technical College entrance. BBC cameraman Les Leach, was the only one to film his arrival. ITN doggedly hovered above the street while those of us on the ground hanging from bought-up window positions, straining to view everything, saw nothing but the arrival and departure of a very elegant bus.

Cromwell Street was ignited once more. Its inhabitants, in an almost carnival mood, spilled out of doorways, determined not to miss the circus of justice as it made its way to the Big Top tent towering over the small back garden. Most of the floating population who inhabited the area during the dramatic days of 1994 had sailed off to other ports of call. Some of the characters we had come to know, sometimes fear, had moved on, either to improve their lot or in haste to avoid unpaid landlords or avoid the law. Now we were greeted by new faces on the street, out to enjoy the autumnal sunshine.

They sat on doorsteps, laughing, chatting, drinking tea, sipping coke, hung from window sills, lounged against walls. Having seen the courtroom circus arrive, they wanted the value for money of watching it leave. Amid all the street activity, a gentleman of African origin, resplendent in tweed jacket and cavalry twill trousers, walked along St Michael's Square bearing a large gilt-framed painting in one hand, at the same time wielding a torch with which he flashed morse code-like signals to the circling overhead aircraft.

Unchallenged by police or locals, he stood in the centre of the road tapping out his messages of light. Having satisfied himself that contact had been made with the aviators, he put away his lamp and handed out gold-embossed business cards to anyone showing the slightest interest. The calling card read:

Artist.
Oils On Canvas Or Panel.
From Photograph Or Life.
McKenzley Arthur Lampkin,
Albion Villa, Gloucester.

Shortly after this comic cuts caper, Mr Justice Mantell followed by the bus-load jury left Cromwell Street for the relative sanity of Winchester.

Holding court

For Rose West, the long wait was nearing its end as the jury approached decision time. Since the first clods of earth had been turned by police in her Gloucester garden, it had taken 637 days to bring her to trial. After facing seven weeks of harrowing facts and details, occasionally laced with the odd pinch of fiction, the jury had reached the end of the legal argument. The climax to this crime of crimes was nigh when the judge delivered his summing up and sent the seven men and four women out to deliberate on the verdict.

But like everything else connected with this morose tale, it was not to be straightforward. Central Television gave me the opportunity to cover the last day of the trial, which everyone assumed would be on Monday November 20th. This turned out to be wrong by two days. With the jury out, for the first time in nearly two months the media could relax. There would be ample warning of the jury's return, so cameras were dismounted, notebooks stowed and the press pack retired to the warmth of the court corridors and its café. As ever, conversation revolved around the case and its outcome. Would she be found guilty on all counts? How long would she get? Might she change her plea? There were no bets on Rosemary West walking free. To a man, the opinion was that she would be found guilty, but a few side bets were organised as to when the jurors would return the verdict. Most backed a Tuesday decision, placing pound coins against the actual hour. Those betting on Wednesday lunchtime scooped up the winnings.

After a night in their secret hotel, the jury returned on Tuesday morning to proclaim the defendant guilty on three charges of murder. There would be another evening's luxury accommodation and a further twelve hours' deliberation before Rose West was to know her fate. At midday on Wednesday November 22nd, the eleven jurors delivered a guilty verdict on the seven remaining murder charges. A stunned Rose West stared motionless as the public gallery burst into cheers. It was all over. Outside the court there was mayhem. The timing of the verdict coincided with lunchtime bulletins and each TV channel was desperate to make the slot.

Instructions were yelled over mobile phones, directives taken in mad panic ... it was all 'camera, lights, action'! Distanced from this clamour, my brief was important but relatively simple. Shortly after the jury's dismissal I left the courthouse pandemonium to film an end-of-trial exclusive interview with Fred West's daughter, Anne Marie. The whole exercise was to be carried out in complete secrecy to avoid interference from opposition media. After a 15-mile journey, Central reporter Ken Goodwin and I were sitting in the car in a narrow country lane, awaiting Anne Marie's arrival at the prearranged location. To kill time, we turned into a news bulletin on the car radio and heard the announcement: " "Police are anxious to trace nine more women known to have frequented 25 Cromwell Street".

The news item continued with brief descriptions, vague details and approximate dates. No more, no less. The Cromwell Street house locked, the Winchester trial closed yet the Investigation, still open. Anne Marie climbed, ashen-faced, from her car to meet us, the strain of the last few weeks etched on her features. Although visibly shaking, she was the same controlled Anne Marie I had filmed in April at her mother's funeral, calling up an inner strength to face that ordeal. Here she was, again preparing to express complex emotions to a camera, only minutes after being plucked from one of the most traumatic experiences of her life. Ken handled the delicate situation with a fine balance and gentle decorum. The wrong intonation, the clumsily-phrased question or a sense of personal intrusion and all would be lost. He did not put a foot wrong ... nor did Anne Marie.

Silver link

The following morning, every one of the national titles splashed the outcome of the trial along with pages of background material—a torrent of words they had been writing and honing since Fred and Rose West's very first court remand. Armed with a verdict of guilt, they could now publish all the bought-up stories and explicit details, unhindered by judicial restraints. The papers had a field day. Though overdosed on Cromwell Street, their readers pored over each lurid line, digested every shocking fact and some fiction.

Several of the papers, while describing his acts of depravity, commented that the kindest thing Fred West did was to admit to killing Mary Bastholm. This was not true. He may have mentioned it in passing to members of his family, possibly boasted of his involvement to those who wished to listen to his rantings. However, as far as the police were concerned, despite many hours of questioning about this and other crimes, he never once to the police accepted responsibility for Mary's demise. His inquisitors were certain that he knew more that he was admitting but, for some strange reason known only to himself, he denied any guilt regarding Mary. Without hard facts the police could do little but leave the file open on the vanishing of the pretty teenager. Doreen Bastholm died many years ago—a grieving mother gone to her grave with the mystery of her missing daughter unsolved. Doreen's husband, Christian, survived her and at the end of the Rose West trial was in his eighty-seventh year, living with his thoughts in the care of a Gloucester nursing home. He would never speak of his lost girl. The couple had three children, Martin, Peter and Mary. The age gap between each offspring was such they would never be really close. Martin, four years older than his younger brother, emigrated to Australia when Mary was a child and he kept in touch only by letter. The pattern repeated itself when Peter left home at sixteen, enlisting with three of his friends into the Royal Navy, leaving eight-year-old Mary at home with mum and dad. He returned to Gloucester during occasional spells of leave but never really got to know his young sister—their worlds too far apart, a family fragmented by age and distance. As her brother sailed the seas, Mary grew into a teenager attending Linden Road Senior School.

A seemingly contented young girl, Mary was happy at home and school and pleased also to have a boyfriend, Tim Merrett, who lived in the village of Hardwicke, three miles from Gloucester city centre. Like many sailors who travel the world, Mary's brother Peter had found love in his home town, where he met his future wife, Denise. After the honeymoon, Peter returned to sea while his young wife developed ties with her new-found family, finding ready companionship with her husband's sister.

It was natural that the two young women, brought together by a long-distance marriage, would become very close. So much so, that years after Mary vanished, Peter's wife declined to take part in any discussion regarding Mary's disappearance. Her memories of those terrible days were too painful to talk about. It is not difficult to imagine the tension in the Bastholm household during the months of anguish. Mary's middle-aged parents, at first alarmed by their daughter's late time-keeping, their anxieties heightened by fear and dread as the police inquiries became more urgent.

Police frogmen trawled local waterways and scores of officers searched undergrowth and dockside outbuildings to no avail. The gravity of the situation hit them with news that Scotland Yard had been called in to aid the local force, while local and national papers, in tandem with TV news programmes, made nationwide appeals for sightings and information.

Amid these troubles, with her husband thousands of miles away, Peter's young wife Denise, did what she could to console her distraught parents-in-law, an unenviable task even for the most experienced of counsellors.

Meanwhile, Peter Bastholm was on shore leave enjoying a few pints with his shipmates in the sweltering heat of Singapore. As he strode up the gangplank after a night on the town, the ship's officer of the day confronted him with an urgent signal. 'Sister Mary missing—parents distressed'. It was decided he should be sent home urgently and he made the twenty-hour compassionate leave flight to RAF Brize Norton in Oxfordshire.

All he had were those five scant words that turned over and over in his mind as he made the long flight home, unaware of the seriousness of the situation for his grief-stricken parents and young wife. It was the start of a nightmare that for him and his family would never end. He would have to wait until he reached Gloucester before he could fully interpret the meaning of the signal that had brought him half-way across the world to his family home.

After retiring from the navy, Peter settled back in Gloucester where he was employed as assistant manager of a local inn. While Denise was silent regarding Mary's disappearance, Peter was the opposite. He was ever ready to mull over events and express his feelings regarding his missing sister. In the very early days he remained optimistic that Mary would one day turn up, blaming youthful rebellion coupled with a yearning for independence as the reason for her actions. But as the years passed, he came to face the fact that she would never return.

In his heart he believed she was dead. Years later, when the events at Cromwell Street emerged, he began to wonder if Mary could have been one of Fred West's early victims. A least five of the women he killed were last seen, like Mary, waiting at bus stops or boarding public coaches. It certainly gave him food for thought, and even stronger thoughts came after he and his wife Denise, were invited to Gloucester police station to examine a hoard of simple jewellery discovered during the searches at the Wests' home.

Many were trinkets believed to have been taken from the bodies of the victims. Among the pile of fashion items lay a heart-shaped silver locket, similar to one worn by Mary when she vanished. She was also wearing the locket when photographed as bridesmaid at Peter and Denise's marriage. This was the photograph issued by the police to the media when the hunt to find Mary began. Peter could not add much to aid police regarding the pendant but Denise was wholly convinced that the locket was the one that had belonged to Mary. But with Fred West refusing to admit he had abducted and killed Mary Bastholm, the police had no positive link connecting the missing girl and him to the tenuous silver clue.

There were several visits by the police to Peter and Denise's home during the inquiry and from their various discussions with detectives, they were left in no doubt that many of the officers believed Fred West was responsible for Mary's non-existence.

Although West maintained his silence regarding Mary, the facts spoke volumes. Five of the young women found buried at Cromwell Street, had, during the early 1970s, set off from British addresses aiming to journey by public transport; none reached their destination. Lucy Partington, Therese Siegenthaler, Shirley Hubbard, Juanita Mott and Carole Ann Cooper. Every one of them, like Mary, was last sighted either waiting at a bus stop or boarding a coach—each unaware that this trip would be their last. Twenty-six years on, crude graves in the Cromwell Street house and garden spoke for those five victims. No grave has yet been found to speak for poor Mary Bastholm.

Unfinished business: 1

To a man, every reporter will talk about his personal 'unfinished business'—the story he or she can never bring to a close. It might be an unsolved mystery, a police case that remains open and unsolved, a victim of murder whose family is denied closure on their grief because the body has never been found. Criminal history is littered with examples of 'open and unsolved' cases, the ones that deny scribes the chance of writing that final chapter.

For me the constant piece of 'unfinished business' that nags away has always been Mary Bastholm— so near and yet so far.

Among the other examples of journalistic 'unfinished business' I have been involved in to some degree or other was the case of the Haw Bridge torso.

The first thing you noticed about Percy Mills was the penetrating eyes overhung with bushy, beetle brows. Next the gravelly voice, as if he sang at night in smoke-filled jazz clubs. Almost the same tone and Gloucestershire-accented voice of the poet Laurie Lee.

Despite years in the chief reporter's chair at the *Gloucestershire Echo,* Percy's interest in the job never waned. He showed as much enthusiasm in his later years as a junior on his first assignment. I once mentioned that I admired his regular column and looked forward to reading it each week. He seemed genuinely pleased at my interest. Leaning over his typewriter, he fixed me with his mesmeric gaze and said: "You know Michael, it doesn't come easy. Every Wednesday I feel like I'm giving birth!". Despite his modesty, Percy knew his stuff—every seven days there would be another 'new arrival' on the editor's desk. Percy was soaked in newspaper ink, it was the fluid that coursed through his veins, a blue-blooded *Echo* man to the last full stop.

Just a mention of the Haw Bridge torso would set Percy recounting the details of his particular piece of unfinished business— the Haw Bridge Mystery. Eyebrows rustling over his sharp eyes, he would set off in full flow about this grisly tale, crammed with the sort of ingredients reporters die for.

The story began in January 1938, when three fishermen hauled in their nets to discover that a body was the prime catch. They had been seeking salmon in the River Severn under Haw Bridge, a riverside hamlet that lies some six miles from Cheltenham. But this was no suicide or drowning, for the cadaver was missing its limbs and head.

This was murder most foul and in those pre-war days, as now, the public were spellbound by such stories guaranteed to make headline news. During the course of the police river-bank activities, over five thousand people flocked to the area, eager to see the macabre scene for themselves. Now Percy had us all in the palm of his ink-stained hand. He told of bringing his bed into the office during one hectic week of 'my inquiries into the crime'. We hung on his every word, he outlining each lurid happening in court, the facts logged almost verbatim in his notepad mind, each revelation delivered with a theatrically pregnant pause.

A few days before the torso was dragged from the Severn, a certain Brian Sullivan was found gassed in his room at Tower Lodge, in Cheltenham's Leckhampton district. While looking into his apparent suicide, the police came across items belonging to a Captain William Butt, of nearby Old Bath Road. On calling at the home of the retired army officer, they learned that he had been missing for days. Further probing revealed that the gentleman officer and the younger Brian Sullivan had been lovers.

By now, Percy Mills was at full steam as he poured out the facts of one of his biggest-ever stories. When Scotland Yard's Chief Detective Inspector Percy Worth, alighted from his train at the town's St James station, a handful of journalists, including Percy, would report his arrival with front page relish. In the next day's

Gloucestershire Echo the headline read: 'Yard chief arrives in town'. The story dominated the news for weeks as rumours suggested that 27-year old Sullivan had brought pregnant society girls from London and the shires to Tower Lodge where his mother, Nurse Irene Sullivan, had carried out abortions for an agreed fee. After the illegal deed, he would then blackmail the girls for more cash to buy his silence.

The rotten scam became known to Captain Butt who, so incensed by his lover's dishonourable conduct, threatened to expose him to the police. And so the die was cast. The captain was indeed silenced— his limbs and head hacked from the body which was then tossed into the River Severn. The head was never found and as such, no formal identification could be made on the grisly torso.

The Sullivans were certainly prime suspects, especially when a bloodstained overcoat, known to belong to the Captain, was discovered under the floor at Tower Lodge. But police were frustrated in their attempts conclude the case as they could not establish a proven identity to the Haw Bridge body.

75 years on, the file is still open on the bizarre case that rocked a prim spa town. No wonder Mills' curiosity was sparked. No wonder he had kept a scrapbook full of press cuttings about the case. It's no surprise that the mystery stayed with him—it was a newspaperman's dream. Society ladies, sex scandals, Scotland Yard, homosexual lovers, headless bodies, blackmail—all the components of the best crime thriller, and all in his own backyard, right on his patch. A tale to tell again and again.

Every decade he could pull out the cuttings and resurrect the dead with a flashback column, breathing new life into a gruesome piece of Cheltenham's history. And he did just that, as only an experienced local hack can. But neither policeman nor pressman was ever able to establish without doubt the identity of the Haw Bridge torso. That was a fact—the unforgettable piece of 'unfinished business' for each of them.

Unfinished business: 2

The Hereford Times was a broadsheet weekly, known in the 50s for its lack of front page hard news. Instead, the outer pages were covered with notices of forthcoming cattle shows, agricultural auctions, farm sales and the famous Hereford Herd Book Society auctions. Among the bidders were many stetson-wearing American and Canadian cattle barons, anxiously waving their catalogues to acquire the prized Hereford stock bulls, later to cross the Atlantic and join the white-faced prairie herds.

This formidable newspaper, despite its lack of reader-grabbing headlines, could boast a fine team of stalwarts to fill the inner pages. Like reporter Hugh Worsnip of *The Citizen* in Gloucester, they were happy with their lot. They lived and laboured in a pretty market town, in fact a city, with the tranquil River Wye coursing through its heart, set in a landscape of green pastures and half-timbered cottages.

These hacks would have no inclination to leave—why search for Camelot, when you already have it? The paper's writers were a friendly media mafia who, in the nicest possible way, had the city carved up.

No arrow could be thrown, goal scored or run made that sports reporter Ted Woodriffe didn't know about. Every Herd Book stock sale, almost the serving of every heifer by the county's magnificent bulls, was known to the rotund, cheery personage of farming correspondent Tubby Court and his colleague Peter Brown.

The low-profile Tony Badman and his junior reporter Liz Watkins were diligent in finding the news content sandwiched between that beefy menu of agriculture and sport. This rural inkwell of scribes, with their loyal readership throughout Herefordshire, needed little prompting to relate their tales of crime and punishment. Just the mention of the oddly-named Herefordshire village of Canon

Pyon was enough to make their eyes light up in the telling of the 1954 mystery of a man named Derek Saville.

He worked as bus conductor for Yeoman's Coaches, a well-established family business in the village which, alongside the farming community, was a major employer in the area. Saville was said to have 'an eye for the ladies'— working the buses by day and chatting up the girls by night.

On Saturday December 7th 1954, Derek spent a pleasant evening drinking with his latest girlfriend at the village Plough Inn. Later, he walked 18-year-old Ivy Woods to her home, before setting off on his bike to his digs a couple of miles away. It was the last time Ivy would see him.

The next day the normally reliable Derek failed to turn up for work. His boss, having contacted Derek's landlady who said he had not returned the previous night, decided to report him missing to the police. The only clue the police found was Derek's trusty bike, left leaning against the railings of the village hall. Of the man himself, there was no sign at all.

18-year-old Liz Watkins, then a junior reporter with the paper, broke the story. Wandering along Hereford's town centre, she bumped into police sergeant Lucas. Prefacing his remarks with the classic: "Don't say I told you", Lucas told her of frantic constabulary activity involving police dogs and searches at Canon Pyon.

Bursting with this priceless information, Liz raced to the news desk with a tip-off scoop to fill headlines for weeks. Despite many man-hours hunting and house-to-house calls, the police were stumped. Scotland Yard was called in but even they drew a blank. By now, the names of Canon Pyon village and Derek Saville were known throughout the county.

Theories and rumours ran rife: Derek had been tipped down a well by a jealous boyfriend ... had been abducted and disposed of by a cuckolded husband ... had emigrated to Australia to avoid fatherhood, had been hit by a tipsy motorist who panicked and disposed of the body.

There was gossip that police inquiries seeking to establish the whereabouts of villagers on the night of Saville's disappearance had had unintended consequences. It was said that several folk claimed to have been in bed, though the bedrooms were not their own!

Many such tales cannoned off walls at Canon Pyon, providing rich fuel for reporters but no solution to the 25-year old bus conductor's last journey. No body was ever found, no person ever charged. For many years, his £25 pound savings in the Plough Inn thrift club remained uncollected. Saville had vanished into the dark of a country night and in so doing, had created a very rural mystery.

His disappearance provided a drama that hit the headlines for months, in fact years, because each anniversary prompted a few nostalgic columns, if only to keep the mystery alive in readers' minds.

Footnote: Fifty years later, in 2007, a man walked into a Hereford police station to give evidence against his late father. He claimed that when he was just seven years old, he had witnessed his father, with five accomplices, digging a makeshift grave on the edge of Canon Pyon village. His father had recently died and this was now his reason for coming forward and revealing the information.

Armed with this new lead, detectives re-opened the case of 'Operation Panda' which they now listed as a murder inquiry. Of the 1950s case files, none survived, so detectives brought in the help of three retired police officers who had worked on the original inquiry. Earth-moving equipment was taken to the site indicated by the informant. The media pack were also back in Canon Pyon although none had experienced the original search.

The media watched and recorded every bucketload of sorted earth and timed the hours of labour the police put in, digging a 60ft x 6ft deep trench at the site, but no human remains were revealed. The detective in charge eventually came to the frustrating conclusion that it was a futile search—all he was doing was digging himself into a deep hole. There was no doubt that the 7-year-old lad had witnessed his father's activity five decades earlier, but his memory of who and where had become confused and faded over time.

The years swallowed up Derek Saville, yet he is still out there somewhere, the ending of his story remains 'unfinished business' for the newsmen.

Unfinished business: 3

Hugh Worsnip was one of those provincial journalists never lured by the siren call of Fleet Street. Never had the urge to join the hubble-bubble of London's newspaper highway. He could not see the attraction the capital held for so many of his colleagues, preferring the peace of Gloucestershire to the metropolitan rat race. Aged 19 he joined *The Citizen* in Gloucester as a trainee reporter and remained faithful to his paper over many decades. Hugh was content to work within the circulation of the paper's readership, establishing himself as a reporter and columnist with a strong following.

Hugh was a goldmine of contacts and had access to inside inormation that would have been the envy of many national reporters. He was the epitome of the 'trusted local man' for whom information on any story would be only a phone call away. He knew his city and its people backwards: they trusted him with morsels (and sometimes three-course meals) of information that constantly fed his column and news pages. There was a time when all provincial newspapers could boast of such stalwarts but those days are long gone. These are fast-moving times in the world of the provincial reporter—now young hopefuls cut their teeth on a weekly, hone their pencils on an evening, add a streetwise edge with an agency and then, like Dick Whittington, seek their fortune in London. A continuing exodus in the quest for bigger money, greater stories and journalistic fame.

But steadfasts like Hugh Worsnip, steeped in the knowledge of their patch, could reap rich crops from the time, patience and concern they had sown over the years. Stoically, they covered fêtes, court cases, council meetings and a host of small local happenings, all without fuss .. confident that one day they will cover the 'big one'.

When that happens, they come into their own, able to quickly draw on a wealth of sources and contacts of KGB proportions. As the story first breaks, they can't be bettered for no outsider can beat their local knowledge. Only later in the game, when the insidious mix of chequebook journalism and greed come into play, would they be stonewalled.

Hugh had been with *The Citizen* for five years and was, by then, a full-blown reporter when Mary Bastholm vanished from a bus stop in the city's Bristol Road in 1968. The unceasing police activity had yielded few clues as to her whereabouts, nothing more than a bus stop sighting of her and details of the planned destination she never reached.

Now detectives turned to the media for help. Hugh had never before experienced such co-operation. Suddenly his journalistic skills and his paper's editions, became an asset to the investigation. Instead of the usual blunt: 'no comment', suddenly a courtship developed between police and press. Photos of the missing girl were issued without question and media meetings took place almost daily. He came to believe that this was one of the first occasions when police saw the real of value of press involvement—maybe prompted by the more streetwise London officers who recognised that the inquiry was at a dead end. The last hope: the press.

Sadly even this attitude, progressive for its time, was not successful. Having set in motion one of the biggest police inquiries in the county's history involving hundreds of man-hours trawling through vast areas of Gloucester city, alive or dead, Mary could not found. For those of us covering the investigations during that freezing winter, her disappearance remained an enigma.

Years later, when Cromwell Street reared its deathly head, Hugh Worsnip, like many of the local newsmen put two and two together and seriously considered a connection. Today he equates Mary as being the 'star of a show' who never made an appearance, and probably never will. He remains convinced that she fell an early victim to Fred West, speculating that perhaps the madman would not admit to Mary's killing because, in some twisted way, he considered her a 'local' and did not want to be tarnished with her loss.

In fact, Hugh is as baffled as everyone else as to why West maintained his silence regarding the teenager. Like Percy Mills' unidentified torso and Liz Watkins' missing bus driver, Mary Bastholm is Hugh's 'unfinished business', an enigma that's stretched over four decades and which, he believes, is inextricably linked to that other titanic story in his newspaper career—25 Cromwell Street.

He was riding the news desk during the 'House of Horrors' climax, receiving phone calls from a multitude of foreign news editors, crying out for facts. They knew exactly where to go in their search, to the fount of all knowledge in such matters—the local rag. Hugh found himself in the eye of a media hurricane of such magnitude, it was assured a place in the annals of his newspaper's history.

Between covering general news stories, writing his weekly column and preparing backgrounds on the Cromwell Street victims, he appeared on four European television networks and gave ten worldwide radio interviews from the relative calm of *The Citizen*'s newsroom. He reeled out detailed facts while coping with crackling phone lines and heavily-accented questions from an endless list of overseas callers.

The most bizarre of these was 'Drive Time Radio' in San Antonio, Texas. A southern drawl over the line told that Hugh would be 'live' in 30 seconds. After just two questions, a commercial broke in, promoting 'Cheap flights to Acapulco'. Reconnected to the Texas newsroom, he managed two more answers, before yet another jingle celebrated the success of 'Hal's local diner'. The shambolic interview stumbled on in this vein until its merciful end—Hugh quite convinced that no Texan would ever make sense of it. They might fly to Mexico and flock to 'Hal's Diner' but they would never have a clue of the horrors that were unfolding in Cromwell Street— not from the dog's dinner of the radio station he had just been interviewed by.

Hugh, now retired, has hung up his signature raincoat and stowed away his redundant typewriter. Yet Cromwell Street and its outcome will never be erased from his memory—it's indelibly etched there. The years may have rolled by, but the fate of Mary remains a hanging question mark in his reporter's notebook.

Collateral damage: 1

In the aftermath of Cromwell Street, many families and quite a few careers were ruined. All the young children in the West household were secreted away from prying eyes. Dispatched to foster homes around the country, they would be gently counselled in an effort to help them erase the past and prepare for the future—maybe one day to learn of Fred's suicide in prison and Rose's incarceration for life. Perhaps one day to ask the reason why ?The uncouth face of news-gathering, coupled with chequebook journalism, tempted some who had strong links with the case to stray unforgivably in their ways. Family, friends, workmates, neighbours ... all had tales to tell, all poured forth fact and fiction into the notepads of eager scribes craving the exclusive. Journalism via the chequebook had already strained relations within the West family. The tabloids had bought up Anne Marie and contracted both Stephen and Mae West while at Much Marcle, Doug West and his family were in the hands of the soon-to-be-defunct *Today* newspaper. *The Sun* and the *Mirror* also spent their way into the homes and photo albums of various cast members in the city's morbid Greek tragedy. The papers wanted the sensational and they were not let down. The outpourings had been prolific. Every twist, every nuance was wrung from those close to Fred and Rose, family scrapbooks plundered for images of the couple and memories jogged for each anecdote. They were split asunder. No family could withstand such a twin-pronged assault of cash and pressure. Fragmented by internal feuds, they became shattered forever when Stephen West spirited his father's cadaver from the Birmingham mortuary. Sister refused to talk with brother and uncle refrained from contact with aunt in the ensuing row that developed over the secret interment. A family that should have been united by their shared experience became divided ever more. In life, Fred and Rose West were the ruin of many families, in death Fred West managed to completely rupture his own.

Collateral damage: 2

Summoned from his downtown office, Cheltenham solicitor Howard Ogden had been chosen by Fred West to act on his behalf. With the door ajar to what would turn out to be one of the biggest cases in Great Britain, Howard was on the threshold of legal history. At the various Gloucester magistrate remands he handled the press scrambles with great aplomb, unruffled by the scrums accompanying his arrivals and departures. He parried leading questions with courtroom-honed skills while providing useful sound-bites for assembled reporters and TV crews. With a direct link to the man in the cells, the world was at Howard Ogden's feet.

But glory was short-lived. It was alleged that Ogden was attempting to market many of the taped police interviews with Fred West. True or not, angered by rumours arising from a *Daily Mail* 'exclusive', Fred dismissed his flamboyant solicitor without further ado. Howard Ogden was now to wait the ending of Rose West's trial before facing his peers to explain his actions. Meanwhile he walked from the limelight and returned to his cramped Lower High Street office to deal with cases of petty crime. Along the way, the elegant, dog-loving solicitor, had made a terrible mistake—and one that could not have been more in the public eye.

Collateral damage: 3

In the classic way of crime novels, Detective Constable Hazel Savage had a hunch about the whereabouts of Heather West. Something did not add up, did not ring true about the way the young girl supposedly left home. It worried away in the astute mind of the officer and eventually her intuition paid off in a way far worse than she could ever have imagined.

Making that first knock on the Wests' front door, Detective Savage was looking into the whereabouts of just one girl. The shocking conclusion would be the discovery of twelve murdered females.

As the inquiry widened, Hazel Savage delayed her pending retirement. Her commitment to the job meant she wanted to see the inquiry completed. At this point her 31 years' service with Gloucestershire police force was marked with a New Year MBE award, a fitting finale to a brilliant career. But the curse of Cromwell Street struck again. Soon Hazel Savage's reputation was to be clouded by allegations that, via a literary agent, she was aiming to sell the book-rights of her Cromwell Street experiences. These facts or fictions somehow reached the media, landing a bombshell in her lap and triggering an internal police inquiry.

Several officers in the force were genuinely sorry for her predicament. She was a popular colleague who, over the years, had earned much respect for her investigative skills. Yet with all the muck and money swilling around the Cromwell Street case, the police could not afford to be seen as anything but squeaky clean and DC Hazel Savage was duly dusted down. Sadly for an officer with three decades of exemplary service, the inquiry found her guilty of discreditable conduct. Her later appeal to the Home Secretary was to no avail—the blot was to remain on her otherwise police-perfect record.

Collateral damage: 4

In the early remand days at Gloucester magistrates' court, the slightly weary figure of a woman was often seen to accompany Fred West's solicitor, Howard Ogden, into court. The press discovered she was Janet Leach, who had been appointed as an 'appropriate adult' to act as Fred West's 'friend' in court. The 39-year-old voluntary welfare officer, faithfully attended every remand hearing and sat in on eighty-four police interviews to see fair play for the defendant during the proceedings.

She became an intimate listener during her visits to Fred West'stiny cell as he confided his feelings and told his lies. During her constant visits she probably got as close as anyone to the mind of the murderer. She was in a unique no-man's-land— immune from the constraints of police procedure and detached from legal niceties.

What Fred West didn't reveal to police or solicitor, he poured out to Janet Leach. She was spellbound by his private disclosures, he in his element as she hung on his every utterance. He told her Rose was in on all the killings. He had made a pact to take the blame should they ever be caught, so that Rose would be able to look after the children. He said that many of the victims died because of the sexual excesses of his wife, another twenty victims were buried on a local farm. He involved his wife, her father and two black men in the acts of depravity practised at Cromwell Street.

Amid all this gibberish fed into the mesmerised mind of Janet Leach, there was another confession she was given on a plate. Fred told Janet that his cell-mate was responsible for Mary Bastholm's disappearance.

These extraordinary possible truths, possible lies came to light when Janet Leach was called as a witness during the closing days of the Winchester trial. During cross-examination, she denied that she was in the pay of a newspaper. Confronted with a probing question from the defence regarding a book contract, she collapsed in the witness box, causing a halt in the trial as an ambulance sped away from court with a stretcher-laden stroke victim.

Forgive us our press passes

The stain of Cromwell Street bled out in various degrees to contaminate the Wests' family, solicitor Howard Ogden, DC Hazel Savage and Fred West's 'court friend' Janet Leach, leaving a blemish on their lives and careers, as if a curse had blighted all who had become snared in the wicked web woven around that stricken house.

It tarnished the media too, for we all stood on that doorway of depravity with various vested interests. A mix of money-grabbing, sensation-seeking, story-chasing, headline-making reasons. In truth, for many, thought for the victims and their sad relatives were not always foremost. They should have been of course, and at times there was compassion, but the drama of events, unfolding hour-by-hour, meant story-chasing was the powerful driving force: sympathy was in short supply.

This is not to tarnish the whole journalistic profession, which has demonstrated genuine concern and understanding on many occasions. The reporting of the thalidomide scandal, for example, during the 1960s, exposed by the battling *Sunday Times* campaign, achieved relief and redress for many stricken families.

Shocking photographs, bold thought-provoking headlines and moving TV documentaries raised awareness of the starving people of Ethiopia, prompting planeloads of desperately-needed food to reach hungry mouths. This is the powerful and compassionate face of news-gathering, reflecting the best of journalism and what it can accomplish. Yet such achievements are often devalued by thoughtless and sometimes selfish acts in the race to get a story, beat a deadline or satisfy an editor's demands.

All those of us operating within TV news and print journalism—a tribal community where no news is considered bad news—have to live at some point, and to some degree, with the white lie and the devious ruse employed in the hunt for news fodder. Scribes, snappers, TV reporters and cameramen—all of us would have no choice but to plead guilty. Otherwise how could you live with yourself?

Flashbacks

I never met her, yet over the years Mary Bastholm has become a long-lost acquaintance, a companion, almost a friend. She was sixteen years old when I first came to know of her—our introduction purely as a result of her mysterious disappearance while waiting for a bus.

I obtained the police-issued photographs of the smiling girl and distributed them to the provincial and national press in the appeal for information. I filmed and photographed the search teams during the hunt for her. I attended press conferences given by the Scotland Yard officers brought in to assist the local constabulary. But like them, I was never to meet Mary. If she were alive today, she would be in her sixties now … possibly a grandmother. Of course there is no proof she is dead. She may have decided just to wander away from her family and friends, believing as teenagers sometimes do, that the grass is greener elsewhere. But her family did not think that, nor many officers in the Gloucestershire police force. Although treated as a 'missing person', the case had all the hallmarks of a murder inquiry.

From the outset, because of Mary's known background, her disappearance was regarded as totally out of character by the local man in charge, Chief Superintendent Robert Mayo. The inquiry was conducted as a murder, despite the absence of a body. Within days, Scotland Yard was called in to lend their expertise to what would become one of the biggest ever police probes in Gloucestershire.

It remained so until the search for Lucy Partington, who vanished from a Cheltenham bus stop five years later. No stone was left unturned, no question unasked in the urgent quest during the winter weather of 1968 to find Mary. The late John Watkins, then a uniformed police sergeant, was on that search, helping in the many sweeps of land and buildings being carried out along Gloucester's Bristol Road and the adjacent meandering canal towpath. Eventually he moved into the incident room to handle the card-indexing system, a key element of policing methods in those pre-computerised days. As the search spread wider by the week, the card collection grew and grew. Eventually, John turned to his home-workshop, where he constructed, from hardboard and timber, a set of 2ft-square trays to hold and file indexing cards that were multiplying by the hour.

Detective Inspector Wayne Murdock, now retired from the force, said: "The names of Mary Bastholm and Lucy Partington are etched in my memory. At the time, my reasoning was that it was very unusual for two young girls to go missing—even five years apart—from bus stops in the same county. I was stationed in the Forest of Dean at that time, so I never worked on the Bastholm inquiry but I was convinced there must be a link". He continued: "Ironically, just a week before Fred West's arrest in 1994, some information came in relating to Mary Bastholm. I was given the task of locating her file and checking certain facts but I never got to finish the work as the file was requested by detectives working on the fast-moving Cromwell Street inquiry. Nevertheless, like many of my colleagues on the force, I strongly believe Fred West was responsible for Mary's disappearance though probably the file will never now be closed."

The cheerful picture of Mary, taken in her bridesmaid's dress at her brother Peter's wedding, was exhibited all over the city, along with appeals for information or sightings. Mary's face flashed on local television news programmes and smiled out from pages of the evening papers but the appeals brought scant response. Psychics offered their services and were interviewed, things were getting desperate, the police were prepared to go down any avenue, no matter how unconventional. The only strong lead the police obtained was from joinery manager, Vincent Oakes. A Gloucester man who, with his wife, lived only two streets away from Mary's parents in Roseberry Avenue, Vincent knew Mary well as she had often visited their home to play with his daughters.

Walking his dog one evening, he had noticed Mary in the passenger seat of a stationary car, chatting with an older man—someone he described as a 'swarthy builder type'. At the time it struck him as odd that the young girl should be in close company with a man obviously so much older. He reflected that Mary's parents wouldn't be too happy if they knew what she might be up to. "There was no cuddling or anything like that" he said. " They just sat there, deep in conversation."

He was to see Mary in the sandy-coloured, bulbous-shaped car on further occasions, including one time when out with his wife. He was tempted to mention the events to her parents but decided to turn a blind eye to what was probably just a teenage lark—that was until she disappeared. In the light of the police search, in 1968 Vincent Oakes made two statements to detectives, describing the encounters he had witnessed in the mystery car. All the facts were duly logged, faithfully entered into Sergeant John Watkins' spreading index system. Acting on new information, detectives made further inquiries but without a name or vehicle registration number, they had little to go on. The valuable but unsubstantiated lead came to a dead end.

After eight weeks' intense activity, with lack of sightings and no further leads, the case started to ease up. Over forty officers had devoted days and nights in the search for Mary yet not once during the two month vigil, had they been able to point a finger of suspicion in any direction. Reluctantly the inquiry wound down, leaving the frustrated policemen and their officers baffled. Nearly forty-five years on and the index and file on Mary Bastholm's disappearance is still open, still unsolved. John Watkins, the former police sergeant who searched for Mary and who carpentered the simple wood-framed reference system that held every known detail of the inquiry regarding the missing girl, had time on his hands after retirement. Time to reflect on those windswept, snowdrift search days, Time for his mind to turn over a million details in the memory. Time to reflect and weigh up the implications of the Cromwell Street investigation. Back then, like his colleagues, John had no clue as to what had become of Mary—the only hard fact being that she'd disappeared out of the blue. In the light of the developments at Cromwell Street, John Watkins was no longer uncertain about Mary's plight—in common with many fellow officers, serving and retired, he now believed she was picked up by a passing motorist .. believed she was killed by the man at the wheel … believed that man was Frederick West.

During February 1994 when Fred West was arrested and charged with the murder of his daughter Heather, his photograph was splashed across the front pages of both local and national press. By then in his 70th year, Vincent Oakes was mesmerised by the shocking news. But what stunned him more than anything was the bold image of Fred West. As soon as he saw the picture he told his wife, and the police, that this was the man he'd seen in the car with Mary twenty-seven years ago.

By his own admission, Vincent had a poor memory for names, but faces he never forgot. Despite the time lag, he was convinced that the 'swarthy builder type' he told police about nearly three decades before, was one and the same man he saw staring out from the newspaper.

Mind bending

An article in the *Sunday Telegraph* led me to 64-year-old Nella Jones. She lived in Bexleyheath, a couple of miles from the Dartford Tunnel. Over the years, Nella had carved a niche for herself by applying her psychic skills to various crimes. The success of her powers had been recognised by the London Metropolitan police force with a commendation for her assistance on several inquiries. Although never acknowledged, on occasions the police do use the services of psychics like Nella, certainly when they are up against a brick wall. Should the medium's help be successful, it will be interpreted in police-speak as 'acting on information received'.

Murders and mysteries, especially if they are long-running, produce many cranks— those who walk unannounced into the cop shop claiming to be the killer, those claiming valuable inside knowledge or clairvoyants offering their mystic skills. Most, if not all, are gently ushered away but sometimes one will stand out above the rest, a presence that in some way commands attention.

Nella Jones fell within that category. In 1974 she was responsible for the recovery of a £1.25 million Vermeer painting stolen from a house in Hampstead, since when police have turned to her time and again for help. She has traced the proceeds of bank robberies, forecast the planting of IRA bombs and used her powers to solve murders.

Nella attempted to help the police during the Yorkshire Ripper case: telling them that the killer's first name was Peter and that he lived in Bradford. She predicted that his final victim would have the initials 'JH' and would die on the 17th or 27th in Leeds. Jacqueline Hill was found murdered in Leeds on the 17th day of the month. Tragically, much of this information never filtered through to the right man, thanks to internal wrangles that blighted the Ripper inquiry from the outset.

With such a pedigree, Nella Jones seemed like someone worth talking to, despite the long passage of time, she just might be able to shed light on the mystery of Mary. With the blessing of Mary's brother Peter, Central TV's chief Gloucestershire reporter, Tim Hurst, and I made the journey to Nella's London suburb home. I am not sure what we expected but everything seem so normal. A front garden, a front door, a hallway into the lounge—just homely normality. No shaded lights, no mystic music, no glass ball. Nella turned out to be a down-to-earth, no-nonsense lady who exuded self-confidence. She was completely unruffled as the paraphernalia of television interview kit was erected in her lounge. She settled down at a table armed with a pencil and notepad and, as the camera rolled, began to talk while sketching onto the paper. The words poured out: "Fred West first cast eyes on Mary when she was at school, he was working there, repairing something, something that looks like a plaque or a board. Oh, he had a way with the girls did that man". Her pencil was teasing out the shape of a crest, similar to the type of commemorative plaque often displayed in schools, listing the names of former pupils.

"She was a good girl Mary, a nice girl. Yes that's where he first got to know her, at school. His favourite colour was blue you know". Suddenly her pencil started again, inching across the paper. "I'm getting an image of water—a sort of river—there's a bridge, not a normal bridge. This is flat, a flat bridge, no hump and a works or a yard, a sort of builders' yard. Fred knew it well, he went there a lot, I can see his van, not a van, a type of truck like a half-van, open at the back." Nella stopped talking and a silence fell over the room as she filled in her drawing, just the slight sound of the camera still turning. The sheet of paper was now covered with lines and shapes representing what she had seen in her mind's eye. She broke into speech again: "Did the police search this area? Did they look underground? They should have done because I'm getting the impression she's under metal, like a manhole cover, a metal lid. Poor girl, that's where she is, near that bridge under an iron covering."

The lead skated across the page as she shaded in a dark, inch-wide square. Looking up from her work, she passed the sheet to Tim Hurst who studied it carefully. Weighing his words with the experience of years, he posed the question: "Have you ever been to Gloucester?" Nella replied: "As God is my judge, I have never set foot in the town". Tim went on: "So if I were to tell you that Mary disappeared from a bus stop, opposite a timber yard that lies adjacent to a flat bridge over a canal, what would you say?". Nella Jones stared in disbelief before burying her head in both hands and mouthing: "Oh my God". The rough sketch of the Gloucester suburb, outlined by a woman a hundred and fifty miles away from a city she had never visited, was eventually fed into Central Television's computer graphics system at the Abingdon studios. When the image was superimposed over an original street map of the district, it merged exactly into the conventional plan that illustrated the canal system, timber yards and Gloucester's Bristol Road. They became almost one and the same. A timber yard and builders' merchant were exactly opposite the scene of Mary Bastholm's last bus stop sighting before her disappearance.

On our return to Gloucester, Tim Hurst and I made a quiet excursion to the site of Nella Jones' drawings. The canal lock-keeper expressed no misgivings when we explained the reason for our visit, leaving us to explore the area at will. But after a reasonable search—including lifting two obvious manhole covers—we made no revealing discovery.

Could Nella Jones have been mistaken? Were her supposed skills a sham? I like to think not. There are several similar bridges, adjacent to buildings, spanning the Gloucester-Sharpness canal between the city and the village of Quedgeley, where Mary was aiming to meet her boyfriend that evening. Laid over a map, Nella's drawing would have loosely connected with any of those bridges. We may have misinterpreted the location through our eagerness to link the images in her mind's to Mary's last known movements in Bristol Road. Could Nella Jones' psychic gift one day in the future day prove to be astonishing. Stranger things have happened in both life and death.

Downfall

You can understand the logic: remove the tumour. Chop it out from the body of Gloucester. The sickness now over, the scars will soon heal. All will be well. With military precision the officers of the city council laid their plans. 25 Cromwell Street, like its victims, was to be disappeared out of sight and out of mind. Now you see it, now you don't. Only then would the wretchedness of its existence be exorcised for ever.

It was a brave attempt but doomed to failure, Gloucester is saddled with Frederick and Rosemary West and lumbered with the House of Horrors. The city will for ever be synonymous with Cromwell Street. There is no surgeon's scalpel sharp enough to excise the evil, no bleach strong enough to whiten the stain. But the operation had to be undertaken. While Gloucester City Council drew up its plans of destruction for 25 Cromwell Street, the hapless owner of the 'for sale' property sited two doors away (the very same one that had been on put on the market at the outset of the inquiry) struck lucky. A 'sold' sign appeared overnight, signalling three messages: the agent's success in finding a purchaser, the vendors' delight to be leaving the district and the fact that memories had faded enough for the word 'desirable' to be used in the 'estate agent speak'. We'd heard the rumours for weeks and knew the end of the 25 Cromwell Street was nigh. It was just the date that eluded us.

Constant phone calls to the solicitor handling the Wests' affairs plus daily pestering of the city council officials eventually gave us what we needed. On Thursday 3rd October, Mike McCabe, the local authority's press officer, hard-pressed by the press called a hasty briefing for the local media. He revealed that demolition would commence the following Monday. Outlining plans of the operation, he slapped a media embargo on details not to be used until 11am on the day in question. Those of us who attended, promised to honour the ban, at the same time wondering how on earth they could hope to keep the secret under wraps over the next four days.

Three provincial newspapers, three regional television stations and two local radio stations plus various council members were all privy to the knowledge. There was no chance of it remaining hush-hush—too many people with vested interests knew about it, only a phone call away from Fleet Street. With relish, the *Daily Express* broke the news the next day. With the cat out of the bag, the media once more descended on Cromwell Street. Police officers were hurriedly scrambled from their beds or from days off, to provide twenty-four hour security cover throughout the weekend. The bobbies showed no resentment to the disloyal press: after all, the leak had yielded valuable overtime.

Three days before demolition commenced, Fred West's daughter, Anne Marie, was given permission to make a final visit to her former home. Dressed in a black overcoat and carrying a spray of flowers, she was led by police officers across the rear garden and into the dank cellar where she lay her floral tribute in memory of the nine young women who had died in and around the property. Minutes later she reappeared, head bowed and visibly sobbing, as she was led gently away from the charnel house.

And so it was that on Monday 7th October 1996, the demolition team swung into action. Scaffolders cocooned the property within a framework of steel while the site was sealed from onlookers behind a ten-foot high plywood surround The whole of Cromwell Street was closed to through traffic, its residents issued with special car permits. Needless to say, the locals were out in force again, mingling with the mass of hacks and cameramen, many of whom had arrived at the crack of dawn. The destruction of the building would, literally, leave 'nothing to be desired'. Every piece of timber was to be removed and incinerated. Every Victorian chimney pot, roof tile and brick was loaded into sealed containers, transported to a secret site, crushed into granules and buried several yards below ground.

Moreover, the two-week long exercise was monitored at every stage by council observers. All this to deter bounty hunters— collectors of morbid memorabilia. And all this to wipe away the smut and shame that had settled over the city since the initial arrest of Frederick West thirty-three months before, on 25 February 1994. Sledgehammers broke open the bricked-up ground-floor windows, letting in daylight for the first time in nearly three years. Then the wooden guts of the house, joists, floorboards, doors and window frames were torn out and jettisoned through the glassless holes into waiting skips. These in turn, as if on some giant conveyer belt, left the site with monotonous regularity, the timber loads destined for a secret bonfire rendezvous. We had to wait until the afternoon of Thursday before we witnessed the demolition proper. A team of hammer-wielding workers clambered over the scaffolding and spread across the roof. Within minutes the valuable chimney pots followed by their brick stacks were dropped into the void below, altering for the first time in a hundred and thirty years the skyline of Cromwell Street. The dusty exercise took just a week—seven days fewer than the original estimate.

There had been no snags and no further shock discoveries within the walls. From the outset, police were confident this would be the case and they were right. On Saturday 12th October the first lorry, loaded with 16 tons of Cromwell Street brickwork, left St Michael's

Square on the one-mile journey to the council landfill site in Hempstead Lane. There the contents were poured into a mechanical crusher and rendered to rubble before being buried ten metres below ground. On that Saturday, thirteen such cargoes were trucked across the city—you could say one lorry load for each of the Wests' known victims … if you count Mary Bastholm among them.

In a bizarre, history-repeating way, Gloucester's solution to the unwelcome House of Horrors was an echo of events that took place twenty years before, at Ekaterinburg, in the heart of Russia. They also demolished a house to expunge a memory … disappeared a building to hide the shame.

Ipatiev House featured large in Russian history. The striking mansion attracted worldwide infamy as the site where, on 17th July 1918, the last Tsar of Russia, his immediate family and staff were massacred by the Bolsheviks. The royal entourage, having fled at the outbreak of the revolution, were apprehended and held at Ipatiev House while the rebels decided their fate. On hearing gunfire from counter-attacking loyalist White Russian soldiers, the rebels spoke of imminent danger, insisting that the family seek protection in the basement for their safety. The Emperor Nicholas, his wife Empress Alexandra and five children, were led to the rambling basement beneath the building. Following them were their family doctor and three household staff who had remained faithful to the Romanovs. Deceived by the seeming thoughtfulness of their captors, the royal group descended the stone steps in complete darkness, only to face a fusillade of bullets and total oblivion. The callous dispatch of the Romanovs on that fateful night was to become a nagging sore on the body politic of the communist state that eventually emerged from the revolution—it was a wound that refused to heal. Ekaterinburg's conscience, burdened with the mansion's evil history, was eased by its destruction. Now some seventy-six years later, Gloucester was following the Russians' lead. Both cities had inherited title deeds to a house of death, the legacy too horrific to accept. Both cities employed the same solution—total demolition. A message from Moscow was sent to the first secretary of Ekaterinburg: 'Destroy

Ipatiev House'. A local official, a native Siberian, issued the decree. His name was Boris Yeltsin. Thus on the night of 27th July 1977, a giant wrecking ball along with several bulldozers arrived at the imposing frontage of the mansion. The following morning Ipatiev House, now a pile of rubble, was carried off in lorry loads and buried in the city's municipal landfill site. The Bolsheviks dispatched all eleven members of the Romanov entourage within the walls of Ipatiev House, the Wests murdered nine within the confines of 25 Cromwell Street. Both properties held the spectre of violent deaths and both met the same end—one an elegant 19th century mansion, the other a cramped, shabby, down-market Victorian end-of-terrace house.

Aftermath

Now it was no more. The Cromwell Street property and its abandoned semi-detached neighbour had been obliterated— the whole diabolic chapter closed for the final time. How often during the past three years had we reached that conclusion? Just over two months into reporting the story, after the house was finally sealed up, we in the media had left the Cromwell Street area thinking we would never return. But of course we did, again and again and again. It was a vital 'prop', in front of which every TV news interview was conducted. We were there when Fred West dismissed his solicitor, Howard Ogden. We returned when Fred West committed suicide. We were there again on the day of his funeral …and again when the jury made their momentous visit to the scene of the crimes. November 22nd 1995 found cameras there once more when the trial ended at Winchester Crown Court … and again for the subsequent unsuccessful appeal by Rosemary West. Detective Constable Hazel Savage's reprimand by her peers would cause us to make another visit. As long as the house was there we would always return, the backdrop scenery provided by its drab façade always a vital aid on the stage of media theatre. And naturally, we returned for the death scene of 25 Cromwell Street itself, the ignominious finale, played out to expunge the memory of everything, anything, Cromwell.

But this drama would have an encore. Those of us who had been glued to the street during the past two-and-a-half years knew in some prophetic way that this story would never quite go away. Even with the house razed to the ground, some instinct said it would not be the end. That gut feeling was to prove correct. Towards the end of November, Fred's elder brother John West, a retired refuse collector from the Abbeydale district of Gloucester, was brought before Bristol Crown Court charged with the rape of two girls during the period when debauchery in the West household was at its height. One of the women was not named for legal reasons, the other was Fred's daughter Anne Marie. She had bravely faced the Winchester trial, watching her stepmother go down for life and now must relive the courtroom ordeal, this time with her uncle in the dock. The start of the trial on Monday 25th November was delayed because bailed John West, had a hospital appointment. After the usual legal preamble, the case eventually got underway, with the two main prosecution witnesses giving evidence of their abuse at the hands of the accused.

Anne Marie's evidence—that her uncle had raped her on at least three hundred occasions during his many visits to the sex-obsessed couple's home—was powerful prosecution material and things did not bode well for the man described by his family as 'a gentle giant'. Sometime during the Thursday night after returning home from the court, the defendant walked out of his back door, entered the garage at the rear of his garden and hanged himself.

For the second time since his involvement with the Wests, Chief Superintendent John Bennett had to unwillingly accept that a prime defendant had strangled his way to silence. For the second time in eighteen months Bennett had to conduct a night-time press briefing on the steps of Gloucester police station, explaining details of the suicide and voicing condolences to a dead man's family—a man inextricably linked to the Cromwell Street affair. Like his brother

Fred, John West cheated justice. True, he may have been proved innocent, but we shall never know because he chose the noose rather than the jury to decide his fate. It is ironic that these two brothers, both charged with heinous crimes, were never judged. They died innocent men in the eyes of the law. The police had always hoped that, after a few years inside, Fred West might be persuaded to shed light on other mysteries, including the whereabouts of Mary Bastholm. But his death-by-hanging quashed that possibility. The mantle was to fall on John West who, if found guilty, might also one day provide further insight into the Wests' crimes. But with his suicide, all hope of such help died with him.

The following day, in order to illustrate the headline-making events of the previous night, there was only one place to go—Cromwell Street. As we always knew we would, we returned. Now with the house gone, there was no 'background' … only the blue-grey hoarding remained, constructed with special viewing holes to allow passers-by to peer onto the flattened site, to experience a lifeless tract of land with an undecided future. Not many stopped now to squint through the apertures, the magnet of murder had lost its attraction. The domain of the West family was no more, its remains buried out of sight and out of mind. The act of demolition and disappearance had worked its spell.

Foreign beat

Superintendent John Bennett was duly rewarded for his police service and tireless detection work on the Cromwell Street case. He received the Queen's Police Medal in the Birthday Honours List and, along with his team, was given regal recognition for the unenviable tasks they had all undertaken throughout the investigation. Though there were quite a few mysteries left hanging in the air (and they would probably remain so), the royal commendation was a fitting climax to a highly successful police career. There was however one looming task to confront —his retirement. What to do with all those spare hours? John Bennett could certainly hone his skill as an artist if he chose. During the case he had produced the Gloucestershire police force Christmas cards two years running— excellent pen-and-ink drawings of Gloucester and Winchester Cathedrals—the symbols of peace and goodwill drawn while dealing death and despair. But amid thoughts of the future, he was still a policeman with time to serve: still on the beat and soon to tramp another road, another country.

News arrived that bodies of two young girls had been discovered kidnapped and starved to death in the Belgian village of Sars-La-Buisierre. As inquiries around the chief suspect, a convicted paedophile named Marc Dutroux, grew with the fear of more bodies being revealed, the Belgian authorities realised they were confronted with a major investigation, the scale of which was beyond their experience.

Nothing like this had ever happened in peaceful Belgium, a measure of the shock evidenced by the huge pile of wreaths, growing by the van load, at the crime scene. These were local people showing their grief and bewilderment in the only way they knew, with tears and flowers.

In his Gloucester office, John Bennett followed the newspaper reports with a professional interest tinged with sorrow. For him and his colleagues in the Bearland House tower block, their minds still occasionally flashing back over the ghastly images, it must have seemed inconceivable that inside two years, history was repeating itself in a Flemish town. But it was. And the perplexed Belgian police, struggling with events so vile and outside their realm, turned to England and the one man who had first-hand experience—Chief Superintendent John Bennett. Any prospects he may have had of fine artwork and peaceful retirement were shelved as he flew towards a continental Cromwell Street on the other side of the English Channel.

Teenagers

As I type these final chapters in 2013, forty-five years have passed since Mary Bastholm vanished.

During the passage of time, those of her family still alive sadly will have come to accept that she will never be seen again. Of course, they could be wrong. Could Mary, like so many youngsters during the 60s, have been drawn by the bright lights of so-called 'swinging London'? The city with its trendy Carnaby Street allure and Biba fashion, coupled with the exploding pop music culture, was a magnet to teenagers. Is it possible that Mary could not resist the attraction to what was then considered Europe's most exciting city? But there was no history of rebelliousness in Mary. It's likely she played her parents up from time to time, maybe causing the occasional argument, as most adolescents are inclined to do in the struggle to achieve independence. But turning her back on loving parents, leaving them distraught with worry and fear while the police turned over Gloucester in the hunt for her whereabouts, was simply not in her make-up. An act of such selfishness would never have entered her mind.

So what happened to the fair-haired, 5' 3" tall teenager on that bleak winter's night nearly fifty years ago has to be a matter of conjecture—without firm evidence there is no other choice. If you reject the theory that she walked out on her family and friends of her own volition, you are left with only two possibilities. One is that she became the victim of an unknown car-cruising predator—a lone young woman tempting fate at a soulless bus stop, innocently accepting the friendly offer of a lift at face value. It would be a hell-sent opportunity for someone with evil on his mind. Safely in the warm car, she makes small talk .. perhaps about the appalling weather, as the vehicle travels away from the city into the darkness. Taking a journey to only God knows where.

Then again, she may well have known the vehicle and driver who slowed to a halt at that bus stop, happy to get out of the cold and into the warm car because she was acquainted with the man at the wheel. Maybe the man had laid the foundations for this sort of meeting some months before: an older man, a bit of a womaniser, using his rough charm to turn the head of the unworldly teenager, a girl who could not believe her luck when her new friend happened by on that freezing winter night. Though it can probably now never be proved, most of those involved believe the 'friend' was Frederick West.

At the end of the Rosemary West's Winchester trial in 1995, Gloucestershire Constabulary issued the media with two information packs entitled *Cromwell Street Investigation*. The green-covered, spiral-bound booklets, each made up of some fifty pages, listed background details on every officer involved in the case and documented in detail different aspects of the case including plans, photographs and even the financial cost of the investigation.

The packs outlined the early years—the lives of Frederick and Rosemary West from their birth, right through to Fred's suicide and the eventual life sentence handed out to Rose.

This virtual 'diary of death' also produced a shocking 4-page appeal for information on missing persons known to have stayed at, or visited, 25 Cromwell Street at various times between the years of 1973-1991. These facts, hitherto unknown to the press, highlighted the enormity of the task that had confronted detectives during the whole inquiry. They had investigated not just Britain's missing, but other countries' lost folk as well. There were details of nine women—many without names and only scant descriptions, such as:

Person 7 Name - Ingrid (not confirmed). Description in 1978-79, white female, 18 yrs, 5'2", blonde bobbed-style hair, petite, good figure, spoke with a possible German accent. Ingrid is believed to have lived at 25 Cromwell St in 1978/79.

Person 9 Name not known. Description in 1973, white female, 17/20 years, blonde shoulder-length bobbed hair with a flick across the left eye. Said to be of plain appearance and wore little make-up. Spoke with a foreign accent either Swedish or Dutch. She is believed to have lived at 25 Cromwell Street in 1973.

So the list went on, including another Dutch woman as well as the daughter of a USA serviceman based at Lakenheath in East Anglia. It was stressed in the notes that no evidence existed to suggest harm had befallen any of the women listed and there was no significance in the fact that they had yet to be traced. Based on the known activities of Frederick and Rose West, there were some very strong signals jumping out of those pages.

During the 1950s and 1960s, hitchhiking, or 'autostop' as it was known on the continent, was an accepted form of travel, certainly among students and low wage earners eager to see the world. The highways of Europe were littered with young men and women, hopefully waving their thumbs in the air. It was normal practice, so much so that middle-aged travellers with kids of their own often thought nothing of cramming their vehicles with two or three sweaty individuals and their lumpy baggage … after all, it could be *their* offspring wilting under the sun.

Several of Fred West's victims were known to have waited at roadsides or bus stops, Lucy Partington being one. Many were foreign like the Swiss hitch-hiker, Therese Siegenthaler, making her way to the West Country courtesy of 'autostop'. How many others fell under the spell of the grinning, gypsy-haired rover we shall never know. Among the last few pages of police media booklet No. 2 there was a Q & A section .. providing answers to twenty-three questions that the media were likely to ask of the police.

Question: *What is the total number of people that Frederick West is suspected of having killed?* **Answer:** The police do not know. He admitted to the victims at Cromwell Street, Charmaine at Midland Road and his first wife Catherine, in fields between the villages of Much Marcle and Dymock. He spoke of more persons but none of these claims can be authenticated.

Continuing in this vein, the police told of 110 missing people who had been found alive and well as a result of the inquiry and acknowledged the great help given to detectives by The Missing Persons charity helpline. The last question in this revealing tract was:

Question: *Did the Cromwell Street investigation establish any links with the disappearance of Mary Bastholm?* **Answer:** During the course of the investigation into Mary's disappearance, over 250 different lines of inquiry were pursued. Following a complete review of the missing person file which had been retained since her disappearance, over one hundred people who had either initially been seen by the original investigating team, or people found by the current inquiry, were interviewed. Some people in the original inquiry who may have been of assistance were found to have died. Despite these inquires no evidence was found to support arresting Frederick West for any offence in connection with Mary Bastholm, although he was questioned but denied any involvement. The file in relation to her disappearance will be retained and kept open.

This, of course, is police-speak, and the only voice they could possibly offer in the circumstances. They had confronted Fred West regarding Mary's disappearance and he had denied any involvement. They had no clues, no proof and no body, plus a near thirty-year time lapse since the events of 1968. As long as Fred remained silent, the police were stymied, even if privately they believed he was their man.

But though Fred declined to say anything to police about the abduction and killing of Mary Bastholm, he was more garrulous with others. He told his daughter Anne Marie that he had killed Mary and she was buried somewhere in the village of Bishop's Cleeve, near Cheltenham. Significantly, at the time Mary disappeared, Fred West was living at Lakeside Caravan Park in the heart of Bishop's Cleeve.

He also chatted openly, within the confines of his Gloucester police station cell, to voluntary welfare worker Janet Leach, who was a regular visitor in her role as 'appropriate adult'. Among Fred's many outpourings to her during that time was the -boast that he had killed Mary Bastholm. Talking with his son Stephen during a prison visit on another occasion, Mary's name came up again. Also he supposedly bragged of killing several other women the police knew nothing about.

The purported location for these diabolical deeds, if they genuinely did take place, was a deserted collection of farm buildings near the medieval town of Berkeley, some fifteen miles south of Gloucester.

One story for the 'Old Bill' ... another for sympathetic ears. Which was the truth? Was psychic Nella Jones correct in indicating that Mary was buried near a flat bridge and water in Gloucester city centre? Did Frederick West tell the truth to his son Stephen and daughter Anne Marie? Could welfare officer Janet Leach have been privy to a moment of honesty dredged up from Fred's troubled conscience?

Or was he speaking the real truth in the statement he gave to the police, denying responsibility for Mary's death? Wherever the facts lie, there can be no happy ending for the considered opinion is that Mary is certainly dead and the finger of suspicion will always point directly at one man—Frederick West. During January 2012, some 17 years after the start of Cromwell Street inquiry and around 40 years after Mary Bastholm's disappearance, out of the blue, Gloucestershire's chief constable Tony Melville was confronted with an online petition instigated by one Chris Roberts, of Ross-on-Wye in Herefordshire.

The missive, containing 329 signatures, called on the police to excavate the cellar of the Oasis Café (formerly known as the Pop-In Café) in Southgate Street, Gloucester in a search for the remains Mary Bastholm.

Mr Roberts presented several 'facts' in support of his case but these were strongly refuted by Melville in an open letter via the media, addressed to Mr Roberts and the petitioners. He explained why his officers would not be digging up the café. This is the essence of his reply to questions raised regarding by the petition:

Dear Mr Roberts, We have reviewed the information in your letter in conjunction with material we hold from the 1994 investigation regarding Fred and Rosemary West and the 1968 inquiry into the disappearance of Mary Bastholm.

Your letter refers to 'six known irrefutable facts' concerning the relationship between Mary and Fred West and you call on us to explain why the Pop-In Café was not forensically analysed following the discovery of Mary's exercise book in the toilet area in 1994.

It is unusual for us to give the level of detail that follows but we do so because of the scale of public interest and at the request of Mary's family, who relive the trauma of her loss with each public airing of the facts, often intertwined with varying inaccuracy and urban myth.

Petition: Fred was a regular customer of the cafe and knew Mary.
Reply: The 1994 inquiry found evidence of this but it was always denied by Fred West.

Petition: Mary was seen in West's car on more than one occasion.
Reply: There is evidence from the 1994 inquiry which tends to suggest this but it is in no way categoric.

Petition: West admitted to his son Stephen and to Janet Leach that he killed Mary.

Reply: Fred West was and remains the only suspect for the abduction and murder of Mary Bastholm. In interview he denied it. No information of Mary's whereabouts has ever come to light.

Petition: West did the basement building work at the Pop-In Cafe around the time of Mary's disappearance, a major part of this work was laying a concrete floor.

Reply: This is not true. The owner of the café was in possession of the property long before Mary disappeared and no work took place in the building until the late 70s. None of that work was conducted by Fred West.

Petition: West's known modus operandi *was to bury his victims*

Reply: This is correct.

Petition: At the time of West's arrest in 1994 the tenant of the café told police he'd found a school exercise book belonging to Mary, secreted behind brickwork in the toilet area. This book was collected by the police but the Bastholm family were not informed of its discovery.

Reply: The tenant contacted police in 1994 about a book he discovered amongst junk and rubble in the basement—not in the brickwork. It was an old café diary which was not connected to Mary. It had no relevance to Mary or her family.

On the basis of the above facts it is our view there is simply no evidence to support the idea Mary is buried in that location. A search of the Pop-In Café would be entirely disproportionate and without foundation and I would politely make a request for the petition calling for the café to be searched in relation to

Mary's disappearance to be removed. We have visited Mary's family and they are wholly supportive of this course of action.

Having furnished you with the full facts, you will now be aware some of your information was flawed and is misleading to the people who signed your document.

I agree entirely with the sentiment you express at the end of your letter—that is your desire to find and return Mary to her family. I don't believe there is one of us in Gloucestershire Constabulary who wouldn't want the same conclusion. Yours sincerely, Tony Melville

So there it was in black and white. The third answer in the Chief Constable's letter, confirms Fred West was and remains, the only suspect for the abduction and murder of Mary Bastholm. The teenager was a victim of Fred West and, even without solid proof, the police were not considering anyone else. So one has to be logical and assume Mary's whereabouts will now probably never come to light.

Studies show that two thirds of all those reported missing are under 18 years of age and of those, there are more females than males. Many walk out because of some problems at home but few are equipped to manage on their own. Those who feel they can't go back can quickly slip through the net into a 'grey area' where they are unable to claim benefits or sign tenancy agreements. They can then so easily become the targets of predators without parents or family members to give advice.

All the victims at 25 Cromwell Street and 25 Midland Road, along with the two bodies unearthed in Fingerpost Field and Letterbox Field near Much Marcle were, after exhaustive searches, eventually found and identified and given a funeral. Every family was finally able to lay their loved ones to rest.

For Mary there has been no such ceremony. Forty-six years since her disappearance, there is not even a glimmer of hope of her receiving dignity in death. She is lost. There is no plot for her family to visit, no headstone to mark her passing.

But maybe she is not completely alone: perhaps she shares her unknown and unsanctified resting place with other lost kindred spirits, other teenagers stolen and never to he heard of again. The roll-call is forbiddingly depressing.

13-year-old April Fabb, last seen on her bike in the Norfolk village of Metton in 1969. Genette Tate, also 13, vanished while delivering papers in the Devon village of Aylesbeare, in 1978. Yvette Watson a 17-year-old who disappeared in 1979 from a Norwich hospital where she was having treatment. 14-year-old Charlene Downes who went missing in 2003, followed four years later by 15-year old Paige Chivers—both girls were from Blackpool. These are just five from a current listing of at least twenty-five such girls who have been reported missing over the decades. There has been no sight of them alive or dead, nobody charged with their abduction, no killer brought to book. Maybe they too are in company with Mary, joining the ghosts of the lost children over all time. I doubt that the file on missing Mary will ever be closed and probably I will never know the answer to my own piece of 'unfinished business' the mystery of Mary Bastholm. And yet ….

Postscript

For the first time in nineteen years, in August 2013 I made the journey back to Cromwell Street … a bizarre pilgrimage to revive memories of people and places I came to know during the long hours spent around the area.

Driving along Gloucester's Commercial Road, my gaze was drawn to the former Central Television studio, its once well-known 'sphere' signage now long gone, taken down by a contractor or stolen by a souvenir hunter? One might never know. Now the forlorn and empty premises were waiting for new tenants. The building had once vibrated with news-gathering energy, staffed by a team of prolific cameramen, editors and reporters who produced more news items at the small dockside studio per man and woman, than any other outlet within Central's region. That is not to say that the Swindon office or the Abingdon headquarters lacked talent—not in the least. The fact was that 'the patch' covered by Central's Gloucester studio encompassed Cheltenham, Stroud, Cirencester, the Cotswolds, Hereford, the Forest of Dean and The Wye Valley—an area unique in producing a constant flow of headline-making news items. While Swindon and Oxford had their moments, for some peculiar reason they never yielded the abundance of news stories as the Gloucestershire 'patch'

At the start of the Cromwell Street enquiry the Gloucester office was staffed with four journalists, Tim Hurst, Richard Barnett, Clare Lafferty and Gordon McCrae, two cameramen, Tim Hughes and Graham Essenhigh and one film editor, Derek Oates. There was also back-up from freelance cameramen like myself, who would be called in for last minute stories or breaking news. Major-domo, Warren Dunn, efficiently looked after security, mail, faxes, phones and tea breaks. In all, they were a tight and highly productive professional bunch who daily turned in the goods for lunch and tea-time bulletins. Film editor, Derek Oates was one of the most unflustered operators at the Gloucester office. Working within the four walls of the darkened and claustrophobic edit room, he daily manipulated, switches, keyboard, cables and reeling videotapes to create attention-grabbing and watchable news items.

At the peak of the 'House of Horrors' case, the normally quiet office was often transformed into chattering chaos as reporters and film crews from other UK commercial television stations dropped in to make use of the edit suite and newsroom equipment or to check facts, send copy, drink coffee and use the loo. Whenever there's a major headline news happenings in any of the ITV regions, it is always 'open house' for fellow commercial television colleagues. This collective form of camaraderie and studio use is taken for granted both in the UK and elsewhere in the world for crews on overseas assignments and in trouble spots, proving that even in war, there can be friendship. On that return visit to Cromwell Street, the passing glimpse of the former dockland TV studios brought back so many memories, and with them a sadness that a once great television franchise by name no longer exists—its former staff and freelance operators all now scattered to the four winds.

I will remember Central South for many things, not least the marvellous opportunities they gave me as a news cameraman working in the UK and overseas assignments. But above all, in my peripatetic and somewhat nomadic fifty-year career, it was from Central that I got my longest-ever news assignment—The Cromwell Street enquiry.

The rows of narrow Victorian dwellings still signal 'cheap bedsit land', some still the tatty same, others modernised and extensions added, taking bites out of back gardens. Unsurprisingly, the corner shop, owned by the amiable Asian family, that displayed *The Citizen's* daily billboards during the 1994 police inquiry, is still in business.

Unsurprisingly, the Wellington Arms, a lunchtime lifeline for many journos and snappers at the time, is now forlorn—another boarded-up former pub, frothing ales no longer pulled and windows blanked with sheets of pasted newspapers.

Of Fred and Rose West's home, 25 Cromwell Street and its derelict neighbour, nothing remains—new visitors to the area will find no plaque, memorial or place name to show where the buildings once stood. Walking along a grass-edged pathway leading to St Michaels Square, none will be aware they are stepping where evil beyond belief took place.

Mr Islam and his family are living in the same house, the home where they kindly allowed us to put up scaffolding in the garden to give us a camera's eye view onto the excavations at the West's property. Their home is still pristine .. twenty years ago they were house-proud enough to lay cardboard through the hall and kitchen to protect the floor from our daily comings and goings. The once media-trampled lawn, probably ruined by our escapades, has now been replaced with gravel.

I inquired about 80-year-old Charlie—I never did know his surname. To locals he was just Charlie, the Wests' sprightly next-door neighbour, expert gardener and valuable contact where the street was concerned. Sadly I learned he had passed away some while ago. Looking to the rear of his house, I noted that his beloved once-prolific greenhouses were no more. They had been removed to make room for a three-storey extension and car-parking space. I thought if old Charlie knew of this he would turn in his grave.

The neighbours to the right of Wests' property were the ministers and congregation of the Seventh-day Adventist church. The building is still there, flourishing as a place of worship, the flock still praising god with gusto and voicing the responses with the same zeal as they did 20 years ago, but back then their eyes rose heavenwards—oblivious of the next-door hell on earth.

At the opposite end of Cromwell Street, St Michael's Surgery continues in the business of treating patients, a multi-nation mix of Asians, Europeans and Africans seeking medical relief. One establishment for the mindful tending of souls, the other for the gentle treatment of the sick.

In between there once stood the devil's domain, where certainly no quarter was given either to human feelings or human flesh. Thank God it is no more. The Gloucester City Council came into their own when they made the decision to disappear the dreadful place and grind it to dust. In that one supreme act, the forward-thinking town fathers returned some measure of status back to the City of Gloucester. Cromwell Street has now settled down to what it was before the early February days of 1994. An ever mish-mash of multi-occupancy buildings offering cheap lodgings to students and an affordable stepping-stone onto the housing ladder to the more permanent tenants. 'Desirable district' is not a description anyone would apply to the area yet for many it is hearth and home and the people there are as good, bad or indifferent as in any neighbourhood.

During my sojourn in the area, I came to know and befriend quite a few of the residents and tried always to consider and respect their feelings during the dramatic events that overtook them. Almost without exception, I found the locals kind and helpful, offering hot tea as a respite from the cold, shelter from the weather and a no-charge facility of household windows to capture the ongoing scenes for the best part of a year, Cromwell Street was very much a home for me.

For the best part of the almost two-year long enquiry, strange as it may seem, Cromwell Street, despite the revelations of its awful history, became a sort of second home and community to me. One I shall never miss, but have difficulty forgetting. The mind cannot be emptied of such evil knowledge—the horrible truths will always be lodged there, lessened with time perhaps but never fully wiped clean. The sad memory of missing Mary also remains—as, for me, it will always so do.

Acknowledgements

I am indebted to the following friends and colleagues: author Katie Jarvis who inspired me to continue and gave me the benefit of her experience; journalist Jeffery Weaver, a doyen of the Gloucester criminal courts and keen supporter of my attempts to publish; news & PR man Mike Waring whose memory is the equal of Wikipedia; Jacqui Mills for kindly editing the material; photographer Rob Lacey who designed the book cover; former BBC Points West journalist Graham Gardner, poacher-turned-gamekeeper now Police and Crime Commissioner's media adviser with Gloucestershire Constabulary, who generously checked for accuracy; Andy Jones, owner of 'Crime Through Time Museum', who aided research in certain sections of the book; Hilary Allison, Press Officer with Gloucestershire Constabulary during the Cromwell Street enquiry, who kindly furnished notes of her time as the 'Angel of Cromwell Street'; Detective Superintendent John Bennett, Senior Investigating Officer of the enquiry with colleague Detective Chief Inspector Terry Moore, who kept their promise to pose for photos at the Wests' property the day 25 Cromwell Street was sealed up; all the members of Gloucestershire Constabulary, including the teams of Support Group, too many to mention individually, who put up with my stubborn presence and to some degree accepted me as part of the furniture. I bet they miss the doughnuts! And the numerous contacts invaluable in the daily hunt for news—not mentioned by name but they know who I mean. Thank you.

The list would not be complete without thanks to Central TV's news desks at Gloucester and Abingdon: without their foresight in following every aspect of the Fred and Rose West case and giving me a lion's share of 'being there' on their behalf, this book would not have been possible. There are too many names to mention individually so please forgive the omissions but particular thanks must go to Geoff Barratt, Keith Hutchence, Chris Moore, Laurie Upshon, Karen Thompson, and Phil Carrodus. Thanks to you all.

Lightning Source UK Ltd.
Milton Keynes UK
UKOW07f0757141114

241599UK00002B/59/P